"Do you see what I see?" whispered Lavinia as they approached Selma's house. "Isn't that Selma's car parked in front of the house?"

Peggy tugged at Lavinia's arm, motioning to her to stand still. "Look at the second floor," Peggy whispered. "I see a light up there."

"I told you Selma wasn't dead," said Lavinia.

The women stayed in the shadows. "That's not an ordinary light," said Peggy. "It's a flashlight. Someone's up there. I'm going around back to get a better look. You go around the front. Stick to the sidewalk. I'll meet you at the driveway . . ."

Lavinia turned her head to look up at the house. The only light now visible was the reflected moonlight in the second story window. The ground floor windows were shuttered . . .

"Let's get out of here fast," she whispered, grabbing Peggy's sleeve . . .

DEATH OF A TART

KATE BORDEN

BERKLEY PRIME CRIME, NEW YORK

DEATH OF A TART

A Berkley Book / published by arrangement with
the author

PRINTING HISTORY
Berkley edition / March 2004

ISBN: 0-425-19489-2

Berkley Prime Crime Books are published by The Berkley Publishing Group,
a division of Penguin Group (USA) Inc.,
375 Hudson Street, New York, New York 10014.
The name BERKLEY PRIME CRIME and
the BERKLEY PRIME CRIME design
are trademarks belonging to Penguin Group (USA) Inc.

For Katie

"NICK? I'M LEAVING NOW. DO YOUR HOMEWORK and don't forget to let the dog in. It's starting to rain. Dry Buster off with the old towel hanging next to the back door. Nicky, are you listening to me?"

"I hear you, Mom."

"I shouldn't be too late. No computer games until your homework is done. I left some cookies for you on the kitchen table. Your favorites."

Nick heard the jingle of keys, the slam of the front door, his mom's old car wheezing-coughing-belching before the engine finally caught, the swish-squish of balding tires against the rain-splattered pavement as his mom backed down the driveway into the street.

He looked at the notebook open in front of him. Fifth grade English. What a dorky subject. Write about someone you know. What a dorky homework assignment. Why couldn't he write about baseball? Six weeks until May first and baseball season at the school yard. Who wanted to live in a dorky little town where nothing ever happened and it snowed six months a year? Maybe he could talk his mom into selling the hardware store and moving to Florida.

Yeah, Florida. They could live near Disney World, go watch spring training, maybe even go swimming in the winter. In the real blue ocean instead of the murky old Rock River flowing past Cobb's Landing. That would be so neat. Nick put on his mitt and slammed a well-used baseball into the oiled pocket—whomp, whomp, whomp— while he read what he'd written for Miss Morgan's English class:

MY MOM
by Nick Turner

There's a lot of stuff I could tell you about my mom, but she'd kill me if I wrote it all down.

He counted the words. Twenty-seven if he included his name. Seventy-three to go. Nick groaned, put down the glove, pushed the notebook aside and turned on his computer. Fifteen minutes. He'd play for fifteen minutes.

The walkie-talkie on his desk crackled.

"Hey, Nick! Your mom leave yet for the town meeting?"

Nick looked out his bedroom window, through glistening rain turning to sleet, into a bedroom window in the house next door, where his best friend Charlie Cooper sat at his desk, holding a matching walkie-talkie to his lips.

Nick picked up his own handset. "She just left. Your parents gone?"

"Yeah. They said they wouldn't be back until ten. Maybe later. Are you playing *Crypt Quest*? What level are you on?"

"Eighteen. I got a bomb against the brick wall blocking the exit, but the torch goes out when I push it through the water."

"I aced eighteen after school. Took me two whole days to figure it out. It's really hard. The ones after that are pretty easy until you get to twenty-two. Here's what you gotta do."

Nick forgot about homework, forgot about Buster, forgot about everything but keeping the torch lit as he moved it across the computer screen.

With Charlie's coaching, Nick reached level nineteen as the grandfather clock in the downstairs front hall bonged nine times. He heard Buster banging against the back door, whining to be let inside. Holy crap. His mother would kill him for sure.

Half an hour later, a dried-off Buster snored softly on the braided rag rug at the foot of Nick's bed, paws twitching as he chased imaginary rabbits across a sun-dappled field, a golden retriever's favorite dream. Nick brushed chocolate chip cookie crumbs off his desk and picked up his pencil. His mom always glanced at Nick's homework before he went to school.

> *Stuff about my mom.*
> *She hates waffles.*
> *She gets sad on Valentine's day, but doesn't cry.*
> *She doesn't talk about my dad very much, but that's okay. I was real little when he died.*
> *She works hard at the hardware store. I help after school if I don't have baseball practice.*
> *She worries about money but I'm not supposed to know.*
> *She's the mayor of our town.*
> *I think she's really neat.*

Nick counted under his breath, then erased part of the last line and wrote:

> *I think she's really really neat.*

Done. One hundred words. Exactly what the teacher had asked for. Nick closed the notebook and put it on top of his schoolbooks. He looked over at Charlie's house, but Charlie's room was already dark. Nick turned out his own light and fell asleep to the sound of sleet pinging against his window.

He dreamed he was living in the Magic Kingdom, where it was always summer, always baseball season, and there was never any homework. His mom said it took a lot of faith to make a miracle. But Nick didn't think there was enough faith in all of New England to make anything happen in Cobb's Landing.

CHAPTER 2

THREE HUNDRED AND FORTY-TWO VOTING-AGE residents gathered in the Cobb's Landing grade school auditorium for the annual town meeting.

Peggy Jean Turner rapped her gavel to bring the meeting back to order. "The minutes of the last meeting are approved as presented. Next item on the agenda is the town budget. You all were handed copies when you arrived. Any discussion before we vote on it?"

Cobb's Landing had definitely seen better days. With the closing of the button factory—established by town founder Josiah Cobb before the Revolutionary War, but victim of lower labor costs in Asia and cheaper goods on the world market—Cobb's Landing had become another New England town down on its luck. A town stuck in the fifties. The 1750s. The frame houses had been modernized over the centuries, but the basic styles—mostly Cape Cods or saltboxes with catslide roofs—hadn't changed much since they were built on streets named for trees and plants. On the town square, formerly the village common where livestock grazed, still stood a circular watering trough for horses, converted into a planter for pansies and tulips, now a repository for dead maple leaves and crumpled chewing gum wrappers.

Cobb's Landing was the place where most of the residents had been born, grown up, and married, but a town their children would be anxious to leave.

"Stu? You got your hand up. What's on your mind?"

"PJ, where's that new police cruiser we talked about last year? The one I'm driving now is held together with spit and bailing wire."

Peggy whispered to her friend and neighbor, Lavinia Cooper, a hospital nurse and the town secretary. "I knew this would come up." Lavinia rolled her eyes then resumed doodling on her steno pad.

"Stu, you tell me where we're going to get the money to pay for a new cruiser, and I'll put it back in the budget."

A voice from the back timidly suggested, "We could raise property taxes."

Lavinia handed Peggy a continuous-feed computer printout. Peggy let it unfurl until it touched the floor. "You see this list? Half the town is in arrears on their taxes. People out of work are more concerned about feeding their kids than buying new cars. If they're not, they should be. Raising taxes isn't going to help if no one can pay them."

"Maybe Stu can find a good used cruiser on eBay." A titter swept through the audience.

"Maybe we should sell the town on eBay."

"Like that town in . . . Where was it? Oregon?"

"How much did that go for anyway?"

"Maybe we could adopt an Indian tribe and let 'em open a casino in the button factory." The titter became a roar of laughter.

Peggy's smile faded as she rapped again for order. "Stu, I'm real sorry. Call the trade school. The kids taking auto mechanics said they'd tune up the cruiser for nothing."

A voice from the middle of the room said, "I'll give you a new set of tires at cost."

"Thanks, Bob. Much appreciated. Lovey, put that in the

minutes, will you?" Lavinia dutifully scribbled something incomprehensible on her steno pad.

"What about the raises for the school teachers? We haven't had a raise in three years." The voice came from Virginia Morgan, Nick's teacher and head of the teachers' union.

Peggy poured a glass of water before reaching in her purse for aspirin. Why had she taken on this thankless, no-pay job? To keep Tom's memory alive? He'd been the mayor of Cobb's Landing at the time of his fatal accident with the souped-up waffle iron. Eight years later, Peggy still wanted to throw a brick at the television during reruns of "Home Improvement." She'd completed Tom's term, then kept getting reelected because no one else wanted to run.

"Virginia, here's the deal. We can squeak out a two percent raise across the board for the teachers, if we make a line-item cut." Peggy raised her hand to quell the angry muttering. "I know it's a pittance. I know it sucks. But remember, not one person on the town council, including me, draws a salary from the town. If you want to give the teachers a raise, we'll have to make a budget cut. How about cutting trash pickup? That means all town residents will have to haul their own trash to the dump and three more people will be out of work. Shall we put it to a vote?"

A blast of cold air engulfed the stage. The voters sitting in the front row snapped their heads toward the side door where Chuck Cooper, high school shop teacher and head of the volunteer fire department, had just entered. He stomped his feet and shook ice pellets from his hooded jacket, looking like a shaggy brown bear emerging from a ice-crusted mountain stream, before going up to the stage to put his hand on his wife's shoulder.

"Lovey, PJ, sorry to bust in like this, but we've got a major ice storm going on out there. We'd best table this meeting for tonight, so everyone can get home before it gets any worse."

As the voters gathered their coats, outside there was a

sharp crack like a bullwhip, then the auditorium went pitch-black dark.

Chuck pulled a heavy-duty flashlight from his parka and stood at the open side door, using his light to guide the town residents to the exit leading to the school parking lot. "Drive carefully, the roads are slick."

Clinging to each other for support, the voters gingerly crossed the ice-glazed parking lot, pellets of sleet stinging their faces. Ice-encased tree limbs creaked and fell to the ground in slow motion.

"PJ, we got any salt or sand left?" asked Chuck. "I can get the fire department out to sand the main roads."

"We used the last of it during the blizzard a month ago. I'll get on the phone when I get home. Maybe Grover's Corners can bail us out. We helped them last year." Peggy sighed. "There goes the teachers' pay increase."

"I heard that, Peggy Turner," said Virginia Morgan. "You know this isn't personal, but you're looking at a teachers' strike unless we get something extra in those pay-checks by next fall. I can't keep placating the union members with empty promises. Doesn't look like we'll have classes tomorrow if this weather keeps up." Virginia pulled her scarf tighter around her head before skidding toward her car.

"Peggy, you need a drink," said Lavinia. "We'll open the bottle of Seagram's someone gave Chuck for Christmas. Check on Nick, then come to my house. I'll leave the back door open."

Peggy sat at Lavinia's kitchen table, nursing a weak seven and seven. Hard liquor wasn't in Peggy's budget; when she drank anything stronger than coffee, it was usually beer. "Lovey, what am I going to do? Now I've got a teachers' strike staring me in the face." Peggy put down her drink. "If I ever say I'm running for office again, do me a favor? Have me committed until after the election." Peggy hugged her friend, then went home.

Peggy Jean Turner fell asleep praying for a miracle to save her town.

CHAPTER 3

"DO I HAVE THE HONOR OF ADDRESSING MAYOR Turner?"

Peggy stopped chipping ice off the sidewalk in front of Tom's Tools & Hardware to gaze at the stranger standing next to her.

"You have me at a disadvantage," she replied.

"Max. Just call me Max," said the dapper little man cheerfully. He straightened his red silk bow tie. His receding hairline made his close-cropped white hair appear to be combed to a point on his forehead. With his twinkling eyes and ruddy cheeks, Max looked like a merry old elf. About the age Peggy's father would be, if he were still alive.

On a blustery gray day with temps hovering at the freezing mark—a day when most Cobb's Landing residents were at home putting another log on the fire while their kids enjoyed the luxury of a snow day following the ice storm—Max wore only a suit and tie. No hat, scarf, or gloves. No boots either, Peggy thought as she glanced at his feet. *I wonder how long the spit-shine polish on those expensive shoes will last on a day like this.* She looked up Main Street. There were no cars anywhere on the ice-crusted street. Max appeared to have spontaneously generated, like a mushroom on the lawn after a soft spring rain.

With an engaging smile, Max took the ice chipper from Peggy's hands. "You won't be needing this in a couple of hours." His nose twitched like a chipmunk's. "Do I smell coffee?" Following a chivalrous dip of his head that wasn't quite a bow, Max opened the door of the hardware store and stepped aside for Peggy to precede him.

Inside, he headed straight for the coffeepot. "I always take it black," he said. "Don't mind if I do," he added, helping himself to a cranberry muffin. While sipping and nibbling, Max walked around the small store, eyeing the sparse shelf stock as if he were taking inventory.

"Nice little place you've got here," he said finally. "Did you know this was originally a dry goods emporium? Bolts of calico were stacked on these very shelves."

"What can I do for you?" asked Peggy.

"Ah," said Max, with a twinkle in his eyes and a smile twitching on his lips. "The question is: What can *I* do for *you*? I was at your town meeting last night. Mighty sorry state of affairs you've got here. Cobb's Landing needs a shot in the arm and I can make it happen. Let's go for a walk."

"Why are you so interested in Cobb's Landing?"

"I just took over the Citizen's Bank." Max extended his elbow. "Shall we?"

Peggy and Max walked through the little town from one end to the other. Past boarded-up storefronts and frame houses badly in need of paint. They crossed streets pockmarked with potholes big enough to swallow small farm animals. Finally they reached the former button factory.

The two-story red brick building sat on the bank of the ice-rimmed Rock River. The wooden water wheel that once supplied power to the machinery was stilled. Max took it all in. He saw windows that were broken or clouded with months of grime, crumbling chimneys that needed tuck-pointing, a shingled roof with gaps like broken teeth. A decaying building that was slowly consuming itself.

Max rubbed his hands together gleefully. "This place is perfect," he said. "Absolutely perfect."

"Perfect for what?" asked Peggy. She was chilled to her bones, tired of walking, and tired of humoring someone who could be, for all anyone knew, an escapee from a lunatic asylum. She wanted to go home to her warm kitchen and have a grilled cheese sandwich and a cup of hot cocoa with Nicky.

"Try to see in lights." Max snapped his fingers. A shaft of sunlight broke through the clouds. The ice coating the trees and buildings shimmered like a thousand sparkling fairy lights; the air took on a golden hue seen in tourist postcards of Tuscany or Provence. Cobb's Landing was instantly transformed from drab to radiant.

Peggy sucked in her breath. "Oh, my." Cobb's Landing was bathed in the golden glow of nostalgia and looked the way she remembered it from her childhood. When spring meant hopscotch with Lavinia on the sidewalk in front of her house, playing marbles in the school yard, double Dutch jump rope, kite flying with free kites from the Citizen's Bank. A time when people locked their front doors with skeleton keys, but only when they went on vacation, and kids played hide-and-go-seek on summer nights and tried to catch enough fireflies in a jar to read by.

"That's only the beginning. Set up a town meeting for next Tuesday night. Time is money, Mayor. Ticktock, ticktock. We haven't a moment to waste." With a wink and a wave, Max was gone.

```
╭─────────────────────────────────────╮
│             CHAPTER 4               │
╰─────────────────────────────────────╯
```

CHAPTER 4

AFTER PEGGY CALLED THE TOWN MEETING TO order, Max took center stage. He started his pitch soft and slow, like a practiced angler testing the waters of an unfamiliar stream.

"I'm a newcomer here," Max said quietly. "You don't need me to tell you the history of your town. But I want you to see how Cobb's Landing has changed since it was founded by Josiah Cobb before the Revolutionary War. Lights, please."

The audience was spellbound as they watched two hundred and forty-plus years of Cobb's Landing growth and decline pass before their eyes in about five minutes.

"This is how Cobb's Landing looks today." The image on the screen dissolved to an aerial view taken the morning after the ice storm. The town looked gray and lifeless. Max quickly moved on.

"And this is how it can look tomorrow." Max snapped his fingers. Buds began leafing out on trees, fresh paint appeared on all the houses, new signs hung on storefronts, there were displays in shop windows, even the potholes disappeared beneath newly paved streets. It was like watching an insecure ugly duckling transform itself into a confident beautiful swan.

Max had the room in the palm of his hand and he knew it. A master showman, he had saved the best for last.

The camera slowly panned to the button factory. The red brick building glowed in the setting sun, lights appeared in the polished windows, and wood smoke drifted skyward from the chimneys. The restored water wheel turned slowly, the splashing water a cheerful counterpoint to the chirping birds returning to their nests in the birch, oak, and maple trees surrounding the gurgling Rock River.

The camera zoomed to the building's main entrance. Across the front of the button factory was a banner that read: WELCOME TO COBB'S LANDING, HOME OF COLONIAL VILLAGE.

The residents of Cobb's Landing gasped, blown away by what they were seeing. Then, en masse, they rose to their feet and cheered.

Max grinned like a schoolboy, dipped his head in his little half-bow, then held up his hands for silence.

"There will be jobs for everyone. Colonial Village will be bigger than Williamsburg, bigger than Dollywood, bigger than Wallyworld. It's real Americana. A place for families to rediscover their roots. It will put Cobb's Landing back on the map and turn this town into a gold mine."

This time Max let the applause continue. He'd dangled the bait; now it was time to set the hook.

"We've got to get moving if we want Colonial Village open in less than three months for the summer tourist season. Ticktock, ticktock, people. There's no time to waste. Are you with me?"

A roar of approval filled the school auditorium.

Max beamed. In the emotion of the moment, the tips of his ears turned as red as his bow tie.

He gestured to two people standing off to the side. "I'd like you to meet my top associates. Missy and Ian." The handsome, well-dressed thirty-something pair waved to the audience. "They'll be handing out forms for you all to sign. Your vote for the prosperous future of Cobb's Landing. Sign on the dotted line, then drop the form in the box next to the door on your way out to the parking lot, where you'll find a celebration party ready and waiting. Missy, Ian, meet your new neighbors."

Clipped to each form was a gold pen engraved with the date and the words COBB'S LANDING/COLONIAL VILLAGE. "The pens are yours to keep," Max added magnanimously.

Peggy picked up the pen. It slid between her fingers as if it had been made for her hand. The ink was the color of the bricks in the button factory. Peggy scanned the form—the type was awfully small and hard to read in the dim light—but she signed it with a flourish and was the first to drop it in the box. The rest of the townspeople quickly followed her lead. Max soon had signatures from every voting-age resident of Cobb's Landing.

"Now the fun begins," he chortled softly to himself.

CHAPTER 5

IN THE WEEKS FOLLOWING THE TOWN MEETING, Max became a whirling dervish. He was everywhere, with Missy and Ian close on his heels tapping notes on their Palm Pilots or making calls on their cell phones.

From dawn to dusk, Max prowled around Cobb's Landing checking out houses, exploring abandoned buildings, walking through Josiah Cobb's former manse. Cobb had left his home to the town that bore his name with the provision that the house be maintained as a museum. The town had complied, but the yearly revenue barely paid for the annual repairs.

Lavinia Cooper spotted Max reading inscriptions on the tombstones in the local cemetery. In the evenings Max attended Colonial Village committee meetings in the school auditorium. There were committees for everything from historical research to security to souvenirs. No detail escaped Max's attention.

"Doesn't that man ever sleep?" Lavinia asked Peggy over a brown bag lunch at the hardware store.

"I don't think he needs sleep," said Peggy. "But I sure do. Max is wearing me out with phone calls, reports, committee meetings. He's in and out of here almost every hour handing me lists of building materials to order."

"He's got Chuck organizing the volunteer firemen to paint all the houses and approached me about running a gift shop."

"A gift shop? Really? What did you say?"

"PJ, I've got a full-time job at the hospital, remember? Even if my feet are killing me and I'm sick of thermometers and bedpans, it's a steady paycheck. I've got seniority. Why would I give that up?" Lavinia put down her ham and cheese sandwich to rest her chin on her palm. "Max sure did make that gift shop sound attractive. He said I could double my money the very first season."

"Wait a minute. Who said what?"

"Haven't you been listening, Peggy? Max said I could double my money."

"What money?"

"The money I put into the gift shop."

"I'm all ears, Lovey. Take it from the beginning. Nice and slow."

"Max has a plan. He's going to turn all the abandoned stores here on Main Street into colonial-themed gift shops. You know, the butcher, the baker, the candlestick maker sort of thing. He's even talking about reopening Clemmie's Café, making it one of those family-style restaurants like they have in Amish country."

Peggy listened attentively, nodding every so often while Lavinia spoke.

Lavinia continued. "Everyone will wear colonial costumes and make—or pretend to make, I wasn't real clear on that part—what they sell. Fudge made while you watch, candles dipped in the colors you want. The stuff tourists like to buy."

When her friend was finished, Peggy said, "But what about the money part?"

"I wasn't real clear on that either, PJ. Something to do with a lease and seed money and profit sharing. You know Max. He paints such a rosy picture of everything, you forget the details. Anyway, you're the businesswoman, I'm not."

"I wasn't before Tom died. It was all I could do to balance my checkbook. Now I'm a real coupon clipper and penny-pincher."

"Aren't we all, PJ. You gotta do what you gotta do to survive in tough times. Anyway, Max got Virginia Morgan signed up for some sort of stitchery place. Apparently she makes quilts. I didn't know that, did you? And she's good at it. She's won prizes. Now get this. Selma Thomas is going to run a shop."

"Selma Thomas? Lovey, are you sure?"

"As sure as I'm sitting here."

"What kind of shop?" Peggy asked.

"I don't know. Maybe she'll just sit in the window under a red light the way they do in Amsterdam."

"Lovey, you been watching the Travel channel again on your satellite dish."

Lavinia laughed as she reached for a chocolate chip cookie.

"I wonder if Max knows about Selma," Peggy mused.

"I doubt it. I don't think he's her type." Lavinia brushed cookie crumbs from her fingers. "Gotta run, I'll be late for my shift. Oh, I forgot, can Charlie eat dinner at your house tonight? Whatever you're having is fine. Chuck has a meeting about new signs for the town. All wood with colonial-type lettering. 'Paul Revere's horse pissed here' type of thing. His kids are going to make the signs in shop class."

Peggy laughed. "Sure, Lovey. No problem about Charlie. It's tuna casserole night, easy to stretch. I'll see you later."

Max breezed through the door in the wake of Lavinia's departure. In his hand was a sheaf of paper.

"More orders for supplies, Madam Mayor. Wood and paint for the new historical signs."

"Peggy, Max. You can call me Peggy."

"I'm honored. Peggy."

"Did Paul Revere's horse really pass through Cobb's Landing?"

Max thought for a minute. "Not that I recall. But it's possible. Who's to know for sure? Now about these orders. Ticktock, ticktock. Tempus is fugiting." Max headed for the door.

"Max, wait. I've got one question. Who is going to pay for all this stuff I've ordered?"

Max dismissed Peggy's query with an airy wave of his hand. "Pish tosh, pish tosh. A minor detail. A bagatelle. A trifle. We'll talk about it later. Right now I have an appointment." Another wave and a wink, and Max was gone.

The next morning there were posters plastered on every empty storefront.

COMING SOON—COLONIAL STITCHERY.

FUTURE HOME OF SELMA'S TART SHOPPE.

YE OLDE CANDLEMAKER—OPENING SOON.

WATCH FOR THE REOPENING OF CLEMMIE'S CAFÉ.

A large bulletin board, topped with a countdown clock to the June fifteenth opening of Colonial Village, appeared on the Cobb's Landing town square with a notice announcing a Saturday morning costume fitting at the school auditorium for all town residents.

CHAPTER 6

MISSY AND IAN PAID PEGGY A VISIT AT THE HARD-
ware store.

"Max had to go out of town for a while," said Missy,
fluffing her raven curls with a freshly manicured hand.
"He left us here to troubleshoot in his absence."

At that moment, a fleet of building supply delivery
trucks appeared on Main Street.

"Let me handle this," said Ian. "Is there a loading dock
behind the store?"

He returned a few minutes later with a pile of paper-
work. "Sign these," he said to Peggy, "and I'll supervise
the unloading." Peggy signed.

"Max has such wonderful ideas, don't you agree?" said
Missy. "Colonial Village is truly inspired. One of his best.
You all are going to look so authentic in these darling costumes I've designed." Missy opened a sketchbook. "Take
a look. You're what? About a size six?"

"Eight," muttered Peggy.

"Perfect. You'll be perfect," purred Missy. "Shoe size?"

"Seven."

"We'll get the rest of your measurements on Saturday,"

said Missy, flipping through the sketches. "See what I've designed for the children."

"The kids wear sneakers, jeans, and T-shirts."

"Now they do, but when the village is open, they'd look rather silly and out of place. It would ruin the ambiance. Absolutely ruin it." Missy paused when she saw the puzzled look on Peggy's face. "Didn't Max explain?"

"Explain what?"

"Max, Max, Max," said Missy, shaking her head. "This always happens. Max gets so caught up in the overall vision, I get left with the details. Well, what can you do with a genius like Max?"

Peggy waited for Missy to continue.

"Here's the deal," said Missy. "In order to make this place work, you all will be dressed in costumes every minute the village is open. This is living history. It's a small price to pay for the bucks you'll be raking in. If it's not colonial, it's out. Or out of sight. Got that? Go about your daily lives, as if you were living in colonial times. If you want to have a picnic in your backyard while there are tourists walking about, that's fine. Do it in costume. Max is such a stickler for authenticity."

"I'm not giving up my indoor plumbing," said Peggy.

"Of course not," snapped Missy. "There are certain exceptions for sanitation and creature comforts. But your neighbor's satellite dish has got to go."

"You'll have to deal with Lavinia and Chuck Cooper about that," said Peggy.

"Oh, I will," said Missy. "I've got it on my list." She flounced out the door, tapping on her Palm Pilot.

CHAPTER 7

PEGGY KEPT ANY NIGGLING DOUBTS ABOUT COLO-
nial Village to herself. Her town, the town she'd lived in all
of her life, the town she loved, was on the brink of a new
prosperity and she wasn't going to jinx it with negative
thoughts.

There was no more talk from Virginia Morgan about a
teachers' strike. Even Stu had stopped complaining about
his police cruiser. Knock wood.

Everything was beginning to look the way Max had envisioned that night in the school auditorium. The houses all
sparkled with fresh coats of paint, the shops on Main Street
were being refurbished and stocked with goods, there were
brand-new crisp red-and-white-checked curtains on the
windows of Clemmie's Café (under new management),
and road paving had begun now that the threat of frost was
over for another winter. A volunteer cleaning crew had
scoured the inside of Josiah Cobb's manse from top to bottom.

It was spring in Cobb's Landing.

Peggy played hooky from the hardware store on a Saturday afternoon and went for a walk through town toward

the river. She waved at her neighbors, busy digging in their gardens planting beans and broccoli, lettuce, tomatoes, carrots, and zucchini. She sniffed blossoming spring flowers, and caught the aroma of a freshly baked rhubarb pie cooling on a windowsill.

She heard birds twittering as they carried twigs and grasses to their nests, and the gurgle of the Rock River. The water was still too cold for swimming, but would feel refreshing by the Fourth of July.

The former button factory was undergoing a radical transformation—another of Max's inspirations—into a small hotel, a first for the town. "No strip motel or tacky tourist cabins for Cobb's Landing, no siree," said Max. "This will be a family hotel. Small, but comfortable. Like a bed-and-breakfast. In the summer there'll be fishing and tubing on the river and an old-fashioned swimming hole; ice skating and sledding in the winter. It's a natural."

Peggy returned home from her walk wrapped in a glow of well-being. Nick was waiting for her on the front porch.

"Mom, Mom!" cried Nick. "You've got to do something. You can't let them get away with this." Tears stained Nick's cheeks. He ran to Peggy, wrapped his arms around her, and buried his face. Something he hadn't done since he was a small boy.

Peggy hugged her son. "Nicky, what's wrong?"

"The baseball field. They're gonna tear down the baseball field. Charlie and I went to bat a few balls and there were bulldozers there."

"We'll see about that," said Peggy. Grabbing Nick by the hand, they ran to her car and soon were at the field.

Nick hadn't exaggerated. Parked at first and third base was equipment for plowing under the field.

Peggy drove to the bank, running the red light on Main Street. The bank had closed at noon for the weekend. There was no sign of Missy or Ian and she hadn't seen Max in weeks. She pounded her steering wheel in frustration. "Max, where in the hell are you?"

"There's Missy, Mom." Nick pointed. Missy was just getting into her car.

"Missy!" Peggy yelled. "Wait! I have to talk to you."

Missy sat with her key in the ignition. "Peggy. I'm late for a very important appointment. What seems to be the trouble?"

"The baseball field. Missy, you can't plow under the baseball field."

"Oh, but I can," said Missy in a tone that would frost a pumpkin. "It's on bank land now. A recent foreclosure. I'm sorry, Peggy. Baseball just wasn't around in colonial times. It would be out of place in Colonial Village. Instead, we're using that land to grow Indian corn to be sold at the fall harvest festival. The boys will get plenty of exercise, and paid for their efforts, tending the corn this summer. The tourists will love it. The boys can learn fox, geese, and checkers, a game that colonial children played with corn kernels. They can play hide-and-seek in the cornfield after dark. How's that for a compromise?"

"I think it stinks. It's not fair, Missy. That has been a baseball field as long as I can remember. The boys have been counting the days until the baseball season starts."

"Who said anything about fair? We all have to make sacrifices for progress."

"Missy, do you have children?"

"Me? Perish the thought."

"Where is Max? I want to talk to Max."

"I told you, Peggy, Max was called away on urgent business."

"When will he be back?"

"I really can't say." Missy departed in a cloud of exhaust without a backward glance.

When Peggy and Nick got home, Nick ran up to his room and wouldn't come down for supper. He spent all day Sunday in his room with the door shut. Peggy was helpless to find a way to comfort her son.

CHAPTER 8

MONDAY MORNING PEGGY SAT AT THE COUNTER AT Tom's Tools, opening her mail. Bills, nothing but bills. Bills for all the goods Max had asked her to order. Bills that soon would be overdue. Bills Peggy had no money to pay.

Peggy had no choice but to go to the bank. For forty-five minutes she cooled her heels in a hard plastic chair watching Missy through the glass office wall as she swiveled in her padded desk chair, appraising her manicure while she talked animatedly on the phone.

Finally Missy terminated her conversation and walked out to the lobby to greet Peggy. "Is there something I can do for you?"

"Missy, I really need to talk to Max. How can I reach him?"

"You can't. I've told you that before. He's unavailable, and while he's away, I'm in charge."

"Good morning, everyone." Max sailed in the front door as if he'd been away only five minutes. He was wearing his trademark red bow tie, a blue-and-white-striped shirt, and a white linen suit, which set off his deep, tropical tan.

"Missy! Why is our honorable mayor standing here in the lobby?" He snapped his fingers. "Coffee. Now." He turned to Peggy. "Light cream, two sugars?" He took Peggy's arm and steered her toward his office. "I'm sorry you were kept waiting."

"Max, where have you been?" asked Peggy.

"There were some irons in the fire that required my personal attention. Hot prospects I couldn't afford to lose," said Max. He smiled engagingly. "I left Missy and Ian in charge with strict instructions to take good care of you. They'll answer to me if they were derelict in their duties. Now, what can I do for you?"

Peggy put the folder full of bills on Max's desk. "Max, these bills need to be paid. The suppliers are threatening to cut me off."

"I'm sure we can work something out. A line of credit, perhaps? I can offer very reasonable terms. Say, two percent over prime? Sign on the dotted line and I'll have the money in your account immediately." He handed Peggy a promissory note and a gold pen.

"Max! These bills are for the supplies you told me to order."

"My, my, my," said Max as he thumbed through the invoices. "What a lot of paint and lumber! Who knew it would cost so much? Prices certainly have gone up. But isn't the town looking splendid. June fifteenth is a little over a month away. The media's already talking about the grand opening of Colonial Village. Look at this spread in the Sunday *New York Times* travel section." Max opened the newspaper on his desk, pointing to an article headlined THE LITTLE TOWN THAT COULD. "You can't buy this kind of publicity."

"But, Max!"

Max looked at Peggy. "But what? You agreed to this, you signed for the materials. Everyone in Cobb's Landing agreed to this project that night at the school auditorium."

He flashed a signed form in front of Peggy then slipped it back into his desk drawer. "Whatever gave you the idea that I was financing this project?"

Max is right, Peggy thought with a sinking feeling in the pit of her stomach that felt colder than the iceberg that sank the *Titanic*. He dazzled us all with a dog and pony show, but he never said he was going to pay for it. We just assumed that he was the moneyman. Oh Lord, what fools we've been, Peggy muttered to herself, loud enough for Max to hear.

Max looked very uncomfortable.

"What do you get out of this, Max?"

Max clutched his heart with both hands and moaned dramatically. "You wound me, Mayor, wound me to my very core. How can you suspect for one moment that my motives are anything but pure and unselfish, that I'm thinking of anything but the good of this wonderful town." Max stole a look at Peggy. She wasn't buying his act.

Max slapped his palms on the top of his desk. "I'll come clean. The town gets all the revenue from the tourist admission fees to Colonial Village. The bank makes money from the hotel in the former button factory we now own and the leases on the shops we own. It's a symbiotic relationship. The bank and the town help each other turn eyesores into assets."

"I know what symbiosis means, Max." Peggy was reminded of a recent program on the Discovery Channel about sharks and their relationship with the little fish that fed on the leftovers trailing from the shark's mouth. "You want to put what you just said in writing?"

"I'll tell you what I will do," said Max, patting Peggy's hand. "You pay the suppliers, I'll refinance the homeowners—Citizen's Bank holds all the town mortgages—and credit your overdraft account when the escrow payments are made. It's basic economics, a little matter of cash flow. It'll all sort itself out eventually. Trust me."

"Max, about the baseball field."

"I know all about it," said Max. "A simple misunder-standing."

Missy entered Max's office with a tray of coffee. She did not look very pleased to be relegated to the role of a serving wench. "Missy, you have some explaining to do," said Max. "What's this about the baseball field?"

"Max, I was only doing what I thought you wanted," said Missy. "Who ever heard of baseball in colonial times? You said you wanted Indian corn for the fall festival. I saw that movie about the guy who turns his cornfield into a baseball field. If it worked for him, why not in reverse? Same principle."

"I said I wanted *candy* corn for Halloween. You know Halloween is my favorite holiday. I like to plan ahead." Max put his right hand over his heart. "Baseball is an American institution," he intoned piously. "As sacred as fireworks on the Fourth of July, or even apple pie. Why, baseball was played in the United States as early as 1834, and was nationally recognized in 1846 when the first formally organized game was played. You could look it up."

Max stared at Missy. "What you did was very naughty, Missy. You should know better than to second-guess me. You're one strike away from the minors." Missy looked apprehensive. "We'll talk about this later," Max said sternly. Missy quickly left Max's office.

Max turned to Peggy. "How can I made amends for Missy's regrettable lapse in judgment? Perhaps this will help." He handed Peggy a signed deed to the baseball field. "A gift from the bank to the town. I will personally spring for new uniforms for the team." Max thought for a minute, then said brightly, "We'll rename the team the Cobb's Landing Patriots. Has a nice ring, don't you think?" Max looked very pleased with himself. "Now, about that line of credit. Shall we say ninety days interest-free and two and a quarter percent over prime? Once Colonial Village is open, the money will come pouring in and everyone will profit."

Peggy sighed. It didn't take a rocket scientist to recognize that Max had her over a barrel. She took the gold pen Max offered and reluctantly signed on the dotted line. In red. She was now deeper in debt than she'd ever been in her life. If Colonial Village flopped, she would lose her home and the hardware store. She would lose everything she owned.

CHAPTER 9

PEGGY WAS WAITING AT HOME WHEN SCHOOL LET out to tell Nicky the good news about the baseball field. When Nicky hadn't come home by supper time, she called Lavinia.

"Is Nicky at your house?"

"No, PJ, Nicky's not here. I was just about to call you to see if Charlie was at your house. He hasn't come home from school yet. I'll be right over."

Peggy and Lavinia phoned everyone they knew. No one had seen Nick or Charlie. When the boys weren't home by sunset, Peggy called Stu. He promised to cruise the back roads immediately. Chuck hopped in his pickup to join the search for his son.

The women were too nervous and scared to eat or do anything but stare at the phone.

It was nine when Chuck returned, followed by Stu in the police cruiser. The boys' bicycles were in the back of the pickup, and the boys were riding in the front seat of the police car.

"We found them bicycling back from Grover's Corners," said Stu.

"What were you doing way over there?" Lavinia and Peggy yelled at their sons. "Do you know what time it is? You could have been killed on those roads after dark."

Charlie and Nicky looked at each other. "We went there to play baseball," they said.

Peggy wanted to throttle Nicky. Instead she hugged her son. Then she told the boys the good news about the Cobb's Landing baseball field and the new uniforms. "But you won't be playing there this week, Nicky. You're grounded for not telling me where you were going and scaring me half to death. I was worried sick about you."

Nicky knew better than to argue.

Charlie received the same punishment from Lavinia and Chuck.

When Nicky was safely tucked in bed, Buster asleep on the floor in his room, Peggy sat at her kitchen table and wrote checks to pay all the bills. It was after midnight by the time she licked the flap on the last envelope.

CHAPTER 10

THE NEXT MORNING PEGGY WAS STANDING AT THE counter at the post office, putting stamps on the mountain of bill envelopes, when Selma Thomas sidled up next to her.

Staring straight ahead while pretending to thumb through her mail, Selma said quietly, "Peggy, I need to talk to you. Please meet me at the old cemetery tonight at nine. There's something you should know about Max."

Without waiting for Peggy's response, Selma put a bejeweled finger to her lips then slipped out the side door. But she'd already been overheard by someone else. Someone who didn't want to be seen.

"Of course I'll look in on Nicky tonight," said Lavinia later that day, over their usual brown bag lunch at Tom's Tools, "but Selma Thomas? Peggy, are you out of your ever-loving mind? You know what Selma is. And to top it off, she's crazy. Nutty as a fruitcake." Lavinia paused for a sip of coffee. "It's your life, PJ. Go if you must. But don't say I didn't warn you. I'll bet you an extra-large super-supreme take-out pizza. If she shows, I'll buy. If she doesn't show, you buy. Deal?"

"It's a sucker bet, but I'll take it," said Peggy.

At eight-thirty Peggy yelled upstairs to her son. "Nicky, I have to go out for about an hour. Mrs. Cooper will look in on you. Do your homework. I left some cookies on the kitchen table. Nicky, are you listening to me?"

"I heard you, Mom. You'll be back in an hour. I'll be over at Charlie's house. We're going to look at the moon through his telescope. There's an eclipse tonight. It's our homework for science class."

Peggy drove through the deserted town streets to the old cemetery on the far side of Cobb's Landing. She parked outside the locked iron gates and looked at her watch. Eight-fifty. Peggy made sure her car doors were securely locked. She sat nervously tapping the steering wheel.

The wind whistling through the towering pines silhouetted against the moonlit sky gave Peggy the creeps. Already the moon had a big bite taken out of it. In an hour the moon would be completely shadowed, a dull copper orb gliding silently across the inky sky.

It was one thing to walk through the cemetery in daylight, reading the quaint inscriptions chiseled on the old tombstones—HERE LIES SARAH BROWN, A FAULTY LADDER LET HER DOWN or HERE LIES JOHN TISH, DONE IN BY A BONY FISH—quite another to be sitting here alone in the dark.

The plaintive cry of a screech owl startled Peggy, making her jump. She looked at her watch again. Nine-fifteen. And no sign of Selma. Lovey was right. Peggy had wasted her time on a fool's errand. She turned the key in the ignition and drove home.

"Well?" asked Lavinia, answering her phone on the first ring, waving at Peggy through her kitchen window. "What happened?"

"Nothing. I should have listened to you. Pizza. Friday night. My house. My treat," said Peggy. "Thanks for keeping an eye on Nicky."

"He's still here, in the backyard with Charlie. You want to come over and watch the rest of the eclipse?"

"I'm beat. We'll talk tomorrow."

Peggy fell asleep wondering what Selma wanted to tell her about Max. Whatever it was could wait until morning.

CHAPTER II

PEGGY WAS AWAKENED BEFORE SIX BY A RINGING phone.

"PJ, we've got a crisis on our hands."

"Wha? Whozthis?" Peggy sat up in bed, rubbing the sleep from her eyes.

"Peggy, wake up. It's Stu. I just had a call from the construction foreman at the button factory. He found a body on the waterwheel when he arrived for work a few minutes ago. I'm on my way to the site now. Thought you'd want to know. I've already called the medical examiner."

"I'll be out front waiting." Peggy quickly dressed and phoned Lavinia. "Can you give Nicky his breakfast and see that he gets off to school? I've got to go to the button factory with Stu."

"What's wrong?"

"Stu said someone found a body on the waterwheel."

"Good grief!" said Lavinia. "Who is it?"

"Stu didn't say. I don't think he knows yet. Gotta go. Stu's waiting out front."

"I'll be there in a flash. Chuck can feed the kids and take them to school."

Despite a chilly drizzle, it looked as if half the town was standing on the riverbank gaping at the waterwheel when Stu parked the police car. Lavinia parked her car and ran to join Stu and Peggy.

Stu, followed by Peggy and Lavinia, entered the button factory. They found the construction foreman at the waterwheel.

"I haven't touched anything," he said, pointing to the body.

"Does anyone know who it is?" asked Stu.

"It looks like a woman, but no one I recognize," said Lavinia, standing on her tiptoes to look over Stu's shoulder.

The victim's arms were crossed, with her hands resting on her shoulders. Looks like something out of one of those specials on Ancient Egypt the Discovery Channel keeps running, thought Peggy as she glanced at the victim's hands. She looked again and recognized the rings on the right index finger. HERE LIES SELMA THOMAS, WHO DIDN'T KEEP HER PROMISE. Peggy tried to banish that bit of doggerel from her mind as she stared at the body.

"I think it's Selma Thomas," gasped Peggy, swallowing rapidly. Her legs felt wobbly and she thought she was going to faint. Peggy had never fainted in her life.

"A chair. I need a chair," said Lavinia. "Is there a chair anywhere?"

The foreman dragged over a sawhorse.

"That'll do," said Lavinia. "Sit down, Peggy. Put your head between your knees." She slid her arm around her friend's waist. "It's okay, Peggy. I've got hold of you, you won't fall."

Peggy perched on the sawhorse and let her head drop between her knees. In a few seconds she was feeling better.

"Peggy, that can't be Selma. The face is all bloated and distorted. It doesn't look like her at all. You're imagining things."

"Those are Selma's rings," said Peggy. "I know they are."

"I thought I'd seen everything in my years of nursing," said Lavinia, "but this is too much. No one deserves to die this way. Let's get out of here. I need coffee. PJ, you need strong hot tea with lots of sugar. Stu, I'm taking Peggy home. We'll be at my place."

The children had already left for school, so Peggy and Lavinia had the kitchen to themselves. When Peggy was on her second cup of tea and only crumbs remained on the plate of banana bread, Lavinia said, "What made you think it was Selma Thomas?"

"The rings on her finger," Peggy replied. "I saw them yesterday morning at the post office. Selma was flipping through her mail. Just before she left, she put a finger up to her lips. Like this." Peggy demonstrated.

"I still don't believe it's Selma," said Lavinia, pouring herself a refill on her coffee. "Why did she want to meet you?"

"She said she had something to tell me about Max."

"Max? What could she possibly know about Max? Selma always pretended she knew the secrets of everyone in this town, but I never believed her. Remember what a prissy little snitch she was when we were in school? How she changed. From little miss priss to the town tart."

"Don't remind me."

"Sorry, Peggy. It's ancient history, it's forgotten. I'm sorry I mentioned it."

Stu knocked on the kitchen door. He sat down at the table and Lavinia handed him a cup of coffee. "I think you may be right, Peggy," he said, waiting for the coffee to cool. "The medical examiner found a purse in the river. Inside it was Selma's wallet."

CHAPTER 12

CLEMMIE'S CAFÉ HADN'T YET REOPENED FOR BUSI-
ness, so Tom's Tools became the gossip center of Cobb's
Landing.

Peggy put on the coffeepot, flipped the sign on the front
door of the hardware store from CLOSED to OPEN, and
waited for her first customer. By eleven, she'd refilled the
pot five times and sold eighty-seven dollars' worth of odds
and ends. People felt compelled to buy something while
they drank free coffee and speculated about the identity of
the body on the waterwheel.

However irritating Selma had been while she was alive,
her death was good for the hardware business. Peggy had
no doubt that was Selma's body; but aside from her com-
ments to Lavinia and Stu, she was keeping her opinions to
herself. Shame on me for being so mercenary at a time like
this, Peggy mentally chastised herself as she rang up the
cash register. Then she remembered all those bills she'd
just paid and the whopping bank loan she had hanging over
her head. Tomorrow she'd get the big coffee urn out of the
back room.

Stu popped in about noon to say that the medical examiner had come and gone, and the body had been taken to the morgue. "We have to talk, Peggy. I'll come by your house early this evening. Seven okay for you?" Peggy nodded.

Business was brisk the entire day. Everyone in Cobb's Landing, and a few from Grover's Corners, found an excuse to stop in the hardware store. Everyone but Max, Missy, and Ian.

When Peggy closed the hardware store at the end of the day, she'd made more money in cash sales than in all of the previous week. She dropped her deposit in the bank's night slot and went home feeling fairly optimistic.

The rain had stopped after lunch. In the warmth of the late afternoon sun, Nicky was playing catch with Charlie in the backyard. Buster ran back and forth between the boys, golden tail wagging joyously, retrieving errant throws.

"We're having hot dogs tonight," Peggy called to her son. "Charlie, go ask your mom if you can have supper with us." Charlie ran home to ask permission.

Nicky approached his mother with a solemn look on his face. "Mom, did you really see a dead body this morning?"

Peggy nodded. As much as she wanted to protect Nicky from the cruelties of the world, she believed in always telling him the truth. She squeezed Nicky's hand and they sat in the old wooden glider, slowly rocking back and forth.

"Was it awful?" asked Nicky.

"Yes, it was," said Peggy.

"Was it worse than when my dad died?"

Nicky had never asked about Tom's death before. Peggy took a deep breath. "Nicky, your daddy's death was an accident. I was the one who found him in the kitchen and it was terrible. He was electrocuted. Do you know what that means?"

"Is that like being hit by lightning? We studied lightning in science class. The teacher told us to always stay inside during a thunderstorm. But Daddy was inside, wasn't he? How did the lightning get to him inside?"

"Yes, Nicky. He was inside. He wasn't hit by lightning. What happened was an accident with a waffle iron. He got a bad shock when he plugged it in."

Nicky thought for a moment. "So that's why we always have pancakes. I really like waffles, Mom. Charlie's mom makes them for us, but she gets the frozen kind you put in the toaster. If we got those, maybe it would be all right."

Peggy ruffled Nick's hair. It was brown and straight, like Tom's; not red and curly like hers. "Maybe it would. Put frozen waffles on the shopping list and I'll buy some the next time I go to the store."

"Thanks, Mom!" Nicky grinned, the subject of dead bodies forgotten.

Charlie Cooper ran through the gate in the wooden fence separating the two backyards. "Mom's at work until eight. But Dad said I can stay for supper."

"Charlie, go ask your dad to join us. We'll have chili dogs. You can play ball until supper's ready."

Peggy was finishing kitchen cleanup when Stu arrived a few minutes after seven. The Coopers had gone home after supper and Nicky was in his room doing his homework. Only three more weeks of school until summer vacation. Nick could hardly wait for school to be over.

Stu didn't want anything to eat or drink. He sat at Peggy's kitchen table, took out his notebook and pen, and began to write.

"Peggy, I hate to put you through this, but I've got to ask about your meeting with Selma. If that's really her body, you may have been the last one to see her alive."

CHAPTER 13

"HOW DID YOU KNOW I WAS MEETING SELMA?" asked Peggy.

"I was in the post office," Stu replied. "The acoustics in there are kinda funny. Sound bounces around in all directions. Tell me about your meeting."

"Selma never showed. She asked me to meet her at the old cemetery at nine. I got there a few minutes before nine and left about nine-fifteen."

"Did you see anyone else?"

"No, I never got out of my car. It was too creepy."

"Did anyone see you?"

"How would I know that?" Peggy asked.

"Did anyone else know you were meeting Selma?"

"Lovey knew. I told her yesterday at lunch. She agreed to look in on Nicky last night while I was gone. I don't like leaving him home alone at night, but he's too old for a baby-sitter. I called Lovey the minute I got home."

"How did she know you were really home? You could have been calling from anyplace."

"For one thing, I don't own a cell phone. I can't afford

one. Lovey knew I was here because she waved at me from her kitchen window when she answered the phone."

"Oh." Stu got up and walked to Peggy's window. From there he looked right into the Coopers' kitchen. He sat down again and scribbled in his notebook. "Peggy, we all know there was no love lost between you and Selma. Why would you agree to meet her?"

Here we go again, Peggy thought. I wish Selma had kept her big trap shut and I hadn't been so curious. If I weren't up to my eyeballs in debt, I wouldn't give two hoots about Max.

"Well?" Stu was waiting for an answer.

"If you overheard the conversation at the post office, you know why."

"I didn't hear the last part," Stu said sheepishly.

Oh Lord, thought Peggy. I've fallen for the oldest trick in the book. "Don't you play those good cop–bad cop games with me, Stuart McIntyre. I co-sign your pay-checks."

"Sorry, Peggy."

"Selma said she had something to tell me about Max."

"Go on."

"That's all there was."

"Why would you care what she had to say about Max?"

Peggy sighed. There was no keeping secrets in Cobb's Landing. Better it all came out now rather than later. She took a deep breath, then told Stu the whole story about Max and the bank loan.

"Well, this beats all," Stu said when Peggy was finished. "I don't know what to say. But I can promise you this, Peggy. The people in this town won't let you down."

"Why all the questions, Stu?"

"I've got to do something while I wait for the medical examiner's report." Stu put down his notebook. "Right now all I know is that he found dirt under the victim's fingernails and pine needles in her clothing. The same kind of pine needles found in the old cemetery."

Peggy gulped. "Stu, there are pine trees all over this

town. I've got three growing in my backyard." Oops, thought Peggy, I wish I hadn't said that.

"I won't quote you," Stu said with a smile.

"Is that all? Dirt and pine needles?" asked Peggy.

"One more thing. He estimated the victim had been dead about ten hours when he first examined her. It's possible she died about nine o'clock the night before."

"What did she die of?" asked Peggy.

"He won't know for sure until the autopsy is done. But he said"—Stu consulted his notebook—"she may have died of fright." He shook his head. "That can't be right. It was real noisy in the button factory with all the commotion going on. He probably said she died at night. I never heard of anyone dying of fright before, have you?"

"Can't say I have," said Peggy. "Stu, Colonial Village opens one month from tomorrow. We've got thirty days to get this murder solved or we can kiss the future of Cobb's Landing good-bye."

"I'm on it, Peggy." Stu heard the grandfather clock in Peggy's front hall begin to chime. He looked at the kitchen wall clock, then checked his watch. "Gotta go. I'm late for a date with Virginia."

Peggy's mouth dropped open as Stu ran out the front door.

CHAPTER 14

LAVINIA CAME OVER TO PEGGY'S HOUSE AFTER SHE got home from her shift at the hospital.

"Thanks for feeding Chuck and Charlie," she said.

"Chuck took care of Nicky this morning, it was the least I could do," Peggy replied. "What a day. I was just going to have a beer. You want to split it? There's only one."

"That would be great."

Peggy opened the bottle of beer and poured it into two glasses. She dug out an opened bag of pretzels and poured some into a bowl.

"Cheers." The two women clinked glasses.

"Do you remember the first time we drank beer in this kitchen?" asked Lavinia.

Peggy thought for a minute. "High school. Junior year. My parents had gone someplace. We each had a can of beer we'd taken from our parents' refrigerators and hidden away."

Lavinia giggled. "We drank it warm. Remember how awful it tasted?"

"And you got the hiccups."

"Then we didn't know how to get rid of the empty cans. What did we do with them?"

"We snuck over to Selma's house and put them in her parents' trash can," said Peggy.

"She was grounded for a month. Her parents didn't drink. They thought Selma had fallen in with evil companions and was going straight to hell."

"Do you suppose she ever knew it was us?" asked Peggy.

"Not unless she had those cans dusted for prints." Lavinia smiled. "That was the year you started seeing Tom, and I began dating Chuck. Did you ever think we'd end up marrying the boys we dated in high school and living in the houses we grew up in?"

"No, I didn't. We had such glamorous lives planned for ourselves. What was it you wanted to be?"

"A stewardess," said Lavinia, with a dreamy look in her eyes. "I wanted to be a stewardess. I guess they call them flight attendants now. I wanted to fly around the world, see Paris and Rome. London and Madrid. All the places on the globe." She paused for a sip of beer. "But I never met the height requirement. Then Mama got sick. You know the rest. After Mama died, there wasn't any money. Papa worked himself into an early grave doing double shifts at the button factory to pay the medical bills. I married Chuck, put him through school to get his teaching certificate, then went to nursing school. I can't complain, though. Chuck's a good man, we've got Charlie, we've got a decent life."

Peggy reached over and hugged her childhood friend.

"And I've got you," said Lavinia. "My best friend forever, my neighbor. You sit right here. I'm going to get us another beer."

While Lavinia went home to fetch the beer, Peggy nibbled on a pretzel and thought about her own youthful dreams and ambitions. She had wanted to be a librarian. She loved books, loved the smell of them, the feel of them. Ever since she'd learned to read in the first grade—"See Dick run"—she'd looked forward to curling up in the window seat in her room, opening the cover of a new book. Peggy liked knowing things. She was good at research.

Peggy got pregnant the summer she finished junior college and married Tom on Labor Day. Then her parents were killed a month later in an accident at the railroad crossing. Peggy and Tom took the insurance money and used it to open the hardware store. Nicky was born the following spring. Whatever regrets Peggy had about her life, she would always be grateful for Nicky.

Lavinia walked back in the kitchen with a brown bottle in each hand. "Let's live a little. Chuck said Stu was here. He saw the police car parked out front earlier this evening. What did Stu want?"

"He wanted to know where I was last night. He overheard Selma talking to me at the post office."

"PJ, just because Selma's purse was found in the river, we still don't know that it was Selma's body on the waterwheel. You may think so, but I don't agree with you. That body looked like a bad case of embalming before it got to the undertaker."

Peggy smiled, then grew serious. "The medical examiner said there were pine needles in the victim's clothing and she'd been dead about ten hours."

Lavinia eyed Peggy over her beer bottle. "Pine needles? Is that all? Pine needles are as common here as sand at the beach. Stu McIntyre is out of his gourd. Pine needles. Give me a break. You were home before nine-thirty. I saw you through my kitchen window. I hope you told him. If you didn't, I will."

"I did tell him. He may ask you, though."

"I've known Stu as long as you have. And that goes back to the cradle. He's got to believe both of us. What I can't figure out is why you went to meet Selma in the first place. It's not as if you two were ever bosom buddies. You never cared before about anything she had to say."

"There's something else." Peggy told Lavinia about the bank loan.

"Max put you personally on the hook for this whole project? Of all the nerve."

"Max never said he or the bank was paying for Colonial Village. I just didn't think it through in the beginning."

"We got a letter from the bank today. About refinancing our mortgage. Something about a balloon payment coming due. I'll have to ask Chuck what that's all about. Don't you worry, Peggy. The town won't let you down."

"That's exactly what Stu said."

"See? Great minds think alike." Lavinia bit into a pretzel.

"Lovey, did you know that Stu is seeing Virginia Morgan?"

Lavinia's eyes widened. "Really? I was hoping that Stu had his eye on you."

"You're kidding," said Peggy. "Stu?"

"He's good looking. If you go for the strong, silent type. He's got a job. If you gave him the slightest encouragement . . ."

"Stu?"

"PJ, will you stop saying that? I'm not suggesting you have to marry the guy. Don't you ever get lonely? It's been eight years since Tom died. That's long enough. I worry about you. You can't spend your whole life at the hardware store, running the town or looking after Nicky. You need a life of your own."

"Stu ran out of here like a scalded cat because he was late for a date with Virginia. He's not interested in me."

Lavinia laughed. "On a school night? Virginia Morgan had a date on a school night? It must be love." She poured the last of the beer into her glass. "Well then, what about Ian? Half the women in this town are swooning over him. He's devilishly attractive."

"Lovey, forget it. I've got other things to think about. Colonial Village opens a month from tomorrow. What are we going to do?"

"That body is not going to spoil our grand opening. We've all worked too hard and have too much at stake. Where are those old Nancy Drew books of yours? The ones we read as kids. We'd better brush up on our sleuthing skills. We've got a mystery to solve."

CHAPTER 15

PEGGY WAS BUSY AT THE HARDWARE STORE. BUSIness was booming, even if it was mostly one- and two-dollar sales. I'm probably squandering all my profits on coffee, she thought as she refilled the coffee urn.

The day-old, still-unidentified body found on the waterwheel remained the main topic of conversation. What few facts there were became embellished into fantasy. Rumors assumed the status of facts. The local media began sniffing around Cobb's Landing, eager for a story.

Max swung into action, appearing at the hardware store Thursday at noon. "Ticktock, ticktock. We haven't a moment to lose," he said. "You can't buy publicity like this. A month from now Cobb's Landing will be yesterday's news. Bye-bye baby. Bye-bye Colonial Village. Here's my plan. We're going to have a special invitation-only media preview this weekend, with the opening for the general public next weekend over Memorial Day. We'll give the media a real story."

"There's still a lot to be done, Max," said Peggy.

"You've got to strike while the iron is hot, I always say." Max grinned. "Leave all the details to me."

"How are you going to get the media here on such short notice?" asked Peggy. "The weekend is less than two days away."

"It's who you know and what you know about them," said Max. "It's time I called in a few personal favors." With a wink and a wave, Max was gone.

The countdown clock on the town square moved up from thirty days to forty-three hours. All Cobb's Landing residents were instructed to be at the school auditorium Friday night at seven for costume fittings and final instructions.

Max came back to the hardware store midafternoon to announce the schedule of opening day ceremonies. Ribbon cutting at noon, followed by lunch at Clemmie's Café, the season opener baseball game at two, drinks and dinner at the new hotel, the evening capped with fireworks on the river at nine. The same schedule would be repeated for the public the following weekend.

"Guess who's flying in for the ribbon cutting," teased Max.

"Who?"

"I think I'll keep it a surprise."

"Ma-ax!"

"Oh, very well. I'll give you a hint. But just one." Max leaned closer to Peggy, humming "Hail to the Chief" under his breath.

"Max! You don't mean . . ."

"You didn't hear it from me," said Max, gazing at the ceiling with an air of studied innocence. "Keep it under your bonnet." He raised a finger to his lips. "S-h-h-h."

Peggy felt as if a goose had just walked over her grave.

Cars were banished from the town streets during the hours the village was open. "There will be horse-drawn buggies running a shuttle service from the hotel," Max said. "Residents can park in the hotel lot and ride the shuttle at no charge."

"That's real generous of you, Max," said Peggy.

Satellite dishes had to be covered or taken down.

"You've got to be kidding. What's next, Max? Are you going to remove all the phone and power lines?"

"If only I had time," Max replied. "They should be underground anyway. Very unsightly. Bad for photographs."

Construction crews began working 'round the clock at the button factory, putting the finishing touches on the hotel rooms. Trucks started arriving in town at all hours with goods for the shops, furniture for the hotel.

On the door of Clemmie's Café appeared a chalkboard, topped with the words OPENING SATURDAY. The menu promised homemade clam chowder, oven-roasted chicken, New England boiled dinner, corn bread, and rhubarb pie, apple crisp, apple brown betty, or cherry cobbler for dessert.

The name of Selma's Tart Shoppe was quickly changed to Missy's Muffin Shoppe, all goods baked fresh daily on the premises.

"Missy's Muffin Shoppe?" Lavinia chortled when she stopped in at the hardware store after her shift at the hospital. "That's the best laugh I've had all week. I doubt Missy has ever done more in a kitchen than heat water in a microwave."

"Max has scheduled a baseball game on Saturday afternoon. Nicky will be heartbroken if he can't play. So will Charlie. What do you say we stop grounding the boys as of tonight?"

"Seems fair to me. I'll tell Charlie when I get home."

Chuck and his shop students stopped by with a new swing sign to hang outside of Tom's Tools. "You like it, Peggy?"

"It's great." It reminded her of the old wooden tavern signs she'd seen in history books. "You should sell these to tourists."

"That's what Max said. He gave us the storefront across the street, the space next to Virginia Morgan's quilt shop, rent-free for the summer. We're going to prefab the signs, then paint them to order at the shop."

"What does Max get?"

"Five percent of our gross."

Peggy smiled. Good old Max never missed a trick.

CHAPTER 16

THE SCHOOL AUDITORIUM WAS FILLED TO STANDING room only. Everyone could feel the excitement in the air. Since the closing of the button factory, Cobb's Landing had become a town with a past; with the opening of Colonial Village, it was once again a town with a future.

Max was in his element. He jumped up on the stage with a bullhorn in his hand.

"Good evening," he said. "The costumes are all waiting in the gym. We've set up dressing areas in the locker rooms so everyone can try on their costumes before they take them home. Here's a preview of what they look like."

Missy and Ian walked on the stage, dressed in colonial garb. Missy's vision of colonial clothing wasn't authentic by a long shot, but certainly had style and was flattering to her figure. Under a white apron tied in a large bow in the back, she wore a simple ankle-length brown cotton skirt gathered at the waist; the skirt was topped with an off-white long-sleeved, scoop-necked, peasant-style blouse that displayed an ample amount of cleavage. From underneath the white cloth cap, which looked like a shower cap

with a ruffle around the edge, her raven curls tumbled
loosely onto her shoulders.

But the women had their eyes on Ian. Dressed in fitted
fawn-colored faux-suede pants and matching vest, with a
white shirt open halfway to his navel, he looked like central casting's choice for a second lead in an Errol Flynn
swashbuckler movie. Ian's deep tan, dark wavy hair, and
blue eyes gave him a roguish appearance.

Peggy felt her face begin to flush. Lovey was right. Ian
was very attractive. Peggy fanned her face with her hand—
why hadn't someone turned on the air-conditioning?—and
tried to concentrate instead on the speech she had to give at
the ribbon-cutting ceremony.

Max continued with his last-minute instructions. He reminded everyone that costumes were mandatory during
the hours the village was open; no one was to wear sneakers or sandals. Plain dark flats for the women, brown or
black lace-up shoes for the men. No driving on the streets.
No televisions or radios blaring. No cell phones, beepers,
or pagers in public view. In Cobb's Landing? Get real,
Max, thought Peggy. We can't afford those big-city frills.

Max opened the floor to questions.

"Do we have to let tourists in our houses?"

"No. Your homes are private property. Only the hotel
and the shops are open to the public. Any more questions?
No? Your costumes are waiting. But first, a word from
your mayor."

Lavinia poked Peggy. "Earth to Peggy. Max wants you
on stage. Go on, get up there."

The applause was deafening. The whole town rose to its
feet to cheer Peggy as she climbed on the stage to stand
next to Max.

"It's not me you should be applauding," she said. "It's
your hard work that made Colonial Village a reality. My
thanks to all of you. And Max." Then she added, "And Ian
and Missy."

No one was really in the mood for speeches. They all

wanted to play dress-up. Peggy led the way to the school
gym for the costume fitting.

"Hey, Mom, check me out!" said Nicky.

Max had kept his promise of new baseball uniforms for
the team. Nicky was dressed in dark blue knickers, a
matching short-sleeved shirt, red knee sox, black baseball
shoes, and a blue cap with the name PATRIOTS embroidered
in red. On the back of the shirt were his name and number,
also in red.

"Can I go home and play catch with Charlie? His dad
will drive us."

"Sure. But change clothes first. You want to keep your
new uniform clean for tomorrow."

"Okay, Mom."

Max sailed up to Peggy. "Meet me in front of the hardware store in an hour."

"What's up, Max? It's getting late, we've got a big day
ahead."

"Just be there. You, too, Mrs. Cooper."

Peggy parked her car in her garage. She and Lavinia
grabbed bottles of beer from Peggy's refrigerator and
strolled over to Main Street. The air was soft and warm.
The newly risen moon peeked through the leafy tree
branches; the same trees that only two months earlier had
been coated with ice now formed green canopies over the
quiet streets.

The shops on Main Street were all closed for the night.
New swing signs in front of each store creaked and swayed
in the light breeze. When Peggy and Lavinia arrived at
Tom's Tools, Virginia and Stu were seated on the bench in
front of the store.

"Max told us to meet him here," said Stu.

"He's late," said Virginia, stifling a yawn.

They heard the sound of horses' hooves coming up
Main Street from the direction of the Rock River.

"All aboard," called Max from the front of the buggy
where he was seated next to the driver.

The foursome eagerly climbed into the buggy. They

clip-clopped slowly up Main Street and past the cemetery, where the street became an unnamed road that ascended to a T-intersection with the county highway. When they reached the rise where the roads joined, Max motioned to the driver to turn the buggy and stop.

They looked down at Cobb's Landing, nestled in the valley. They saw their houses spread out in orderly rows on either side of Main Street, in the traditional pre-Revolutionary plan of a seventeenth-century New England village adopted by Josiah Cobb. Lights still shone in some house windows. The pole lights on Main Street formed a glide path toward the river, where the former button factory was brightly illuminated.

Lavinia squeezed Peggy's hand, then turned to Virginia and Stu. "Doesn't it look wonderful?" They nodded in wordless agreement.

"Max, we want to see the hotel," said Peggy.

"It's our next stop," replied Max. "Wait until you see the new amusements I've added for the tourists." Max chuckled softly to himself.

They climbed out of the buggy in the hotel parking lot, then walked down the gravel path leading to the hotel. After a tour of reception, the guest rooms, and the conversation area overlooking the river, Max said, "Now for my surprise."

Next to the newly erected ticket stand, concession, and inner tube rental booths were two horizontal piles of planks with holes cut through them at the top and bottom.

"Strange-looking fence, Max," commented Lavinia.

"That's not a fence, Lavinia," said Virginia. "Those are stocks. They were used in colonial times to punish wrongdoers."

"Go to the head of the class, teacher." Max smiled. "A good photo op, don't you think? Tourists will be lining up here to have their pictures taken."

"What's that, Max?" Peggy pointed to a stout pole erected on the river's edge. At the top of the pole was a long board serving as a lever, looking like an aerial teeter-totter. Suspended by a nylon rope hanging on the river end of the lever was a canvas bosun's chair.

"That looks like a dunking stool," said Virginia. "What's the idea, Max?"

"Great way to cool off on a hot day, don't you think?" Max said mischievously. "They were all the rage in Salem."

CHAPTER 17

PEGGY WOKE BEFORE DAWN SATURDAY MORNING. When she went down to the kitchen to make coffee, she found Nicky, already dressed in his new baseball uniform, eating a bowl of cereal.

"You couldn't sleep either?" she said as she hugged her son.

"Mom! Don't mess up my uniform."

"I love you, too, honey." Peggy looked out the kitchen window. The Coopers' house was still dark.

"Are you nervous about today, Mom?"

"Why?"

"Well, you have to make a speech and everything."

"It won't be a very long speech."

"That's good. Speeches are boring." Nicky caught the look on his mother's face. "I meant the ones on television."

"That's okay, Nicky. I know what you mean. I think they're boring, too."

Peggy took her coffee into the backyard. The air was humid and smelled of rain. Not today, please don't let it rain today. She went back into the kitchen and turned on the news.

"And now the local weather. Today we'll see highs in the upper seventies, clouds moving in from the west in the morning with an increasing chance of showers in the afternoon. Looks like an umbrella day."

Oh, great. Just great.

By eight Peggy was nervously pacing at the hardware store. Her friends and neighbors were busy at their own shops, unloading boxes, rearranging displays, polishing windows that already gleamed. Red, white, and blue crepe paper was being wrapped around light poles.

All cars were off the streets by nine.

Max flew into the hardware store at nine-thirty, cell phone in hand. "Peggy, we've had to move the ribbon cutting up to ten-thirty. You-know-who has a very tight schedule today. The secret service has already arrived. The media reps will be here in half an hour. I need you at the hotel now. Let's go."

"Where's Nicky? I can't leave the store without telling Nicky." One thing Peggy hadn't planned on was finding someone to keep the store open while she was at the ribbon cutting.

"He's at the ball field with his team."

Peggy scribbled a note and left it taped on the front door for Nicky.

At the river end of Main Street a bright red ribbon was stretched across the street between two light poles. A temporary platform, adorned with patriotic bunting, had been erected in the middle of the street. Lavinia and Chuck, Stu and Virginia were already standing on the platform, dressed in their colonial costumes.

"Peggy, what's going on? Who are all those people?"

Peggy shrugged, feigning innocence, as she was pulled away from the reviewing stand by Max.

Secret service agents dressed in black, looking like oversized ravens, were stationed everywhere talking into their wrists.

The media arrived on schedule. Everyone, from camera

man to reporter, was on a first-name basis with Max. He
introduced them to Peggy, then the group on the platform.

Peggy kept nervously looking at the sky. Most of the
blue was gone, replaced by fat, gray clouds. Why did the
weatherman have to be right today of all days?

While Peggy chatted with the media, answering questions about the history of Cobb's Landing—founded in
1757 by Josiah Cobb, a button maker from England; the
first buttons were made from shells; a uniform worn by
George Washington, now in the Smithsonian, was adorned
with special buttons made at Josiah Cobb's button factory—she looked at her town through the eyes of a
stranger.

Colonial Village suddenly seemed like a very dumb
idea. Would anyone really pay money to visit here? Had
the town residents gone deeper in debt for nothing? Peggy
wanted to crawl into a hole and hide. Instead she smiled
and answered the next question.

At ten-thirty on the dot, a large helicopter appeared
above Cobb's Landing. It landed, like a bird returning to a
nest, next to the hotel. Peggy was quickly forgotten as the
media began snapping pictures of the party descending
from the chopper.

The next half hour would always be a blur in Peggy's
mind.

One minute she was shaking hands with the President
of the United States, then he was cutting the red ribbon,
saying, "I am honored to be here today. Mayor Turner,
members of the town council, residents of Cobb's Landing, I commend you for preserving our early American
heritage. May Colonial Village be a reminder to us all of
the values of community spirit and free enterprise that
helped shape New England and our nation." He presented
Peggy with an engraved plaque commemorating the occa-
sion, while tape rolled and cameras clicked. Her speech
completely forgotten, Peggy limited her remarks to thank-
ing the President on behalf of the town.

After a brief buggy ride up Main Street, where

costumed residents cheered the President from both sides
of the street; past the ballpark, where he waved at the team;
around the cemetery; and back to the hotel, the presiden-
tial party reboarded the helicopter and departed promptly
at eleven. The secret service left a few moments later.

Max quickly shuttled the media to Clemmie's Café for
lunch. The popping of the first champagne cork was muf-
fled by a clap of thunder. Rain began to fall in big, fat
drops. By the time lunch ended, it was obvious to everyone that the rest of the day was a washout.

At two o'clock, when the first ball should have been
leaving the pitcher's mound, the media reps were leaving
Cobb's Landing.

CHAPTER 18

ONLY CRUSTS REMAINED IN THE TWO EXTRA-LARGE super-supreme take-out pizza boxes on Peggy's kitchen table. Fast-food chains had yet to find a home in Cobb's Landing, but Alsop's bakery had installed pizza ovens and did a big take-out business on Thursday, Friday, and Saturday nights.

Nicky and Charlie were flopped on the living room floor watching television. Chuck pulled the last three beers from the six-pack and passed them around the kitchen table. "Nothing goes with pizza like a cold beer," he said.

Outside it was still pouring rain.

"Cheer up, Peggy," said Lavinia. "The rain wasn't your fault. You can't control the weather."

"I know that," said Peggy. "I just wanted everything to be perfect. It was bad enough that I blew my speech to the President, but the rain was the final straw."

"Hey, Mom, get in here. You're on television!" yelled Nicky.

"You, too, Mom and Dad," yelled Charlie.

The adults ran into the living room to catch the end of a

network clip showing the President in Cobb's Landing at the ribbon-cutting ceremony.

Peggy grabbed the remote and began channel switching.

"Gee, Mom, we want to watch the movie on the Sci-Fi Channel," said Nicky.

"It's *Return of the Blob*," said Charlie.

"In a minute," Peggy replied.

"Charlie, you and Nicky can go to our house and watch. Nicky, you want to stay overnight?" said Lavinia.

"Can I, Mom?"

"Sure." Peggy smiled at her son. "Don't forget to brush your teeth before you go to sleep."

"You boys have a campout at our house, I'm going to stay here with Peggy tonight," said Lavinia. "If you get hungry later, make some popcorn in the microwave. Tomorrow morning we'll all have breakfast at our house."

The boys ran next door, leaving the adults to channel-surf. In the next hour they caught glimpses of themselves on CNN Headline News, in another network clip, and finally on Fox.

Chuck yawned. "I'll go check on the boys. See you in the morning, honey. Thanks for the pizza, PJ." He kissed Lavinia good night before heading out into the rain.

"I've had enough television for one night," said Lavinia after Chuck left. "Did you ever find those old Nancy Drew books of yours?"

"I've been too busy to look. They're probably in the basement. Or maybe the attic. You know me. Pack rat of the Western world."

"Let's go look for them. It'll be like those treasure hunts we used to have when we were kids."

They started in the basement. In the fifth box Lavinia struck gold. "Our high school annuals. I haven't looked at these in years."

They sat on the floor, flipping through pages, reading silly inscriptions—2 GOOD 2 B 4GOTTEN—laughing over circles, hearts, or daisies dotting the *i*'s in signatures from Tiffany, Kimberley, and Susie.

But it was the pictures that brought back the most poignant memories. Youthful innocence when winning the Friday night game was all that mattered, first crushes on boys not too many years older than Charlie and Nick.

"Look at Selma," said Peggy, pointing at a photo taken at a rehearsal for *Bell, Book and Candle,* the senior class play the year they all graduated.

"Typecasting," muttered Lavinia. "Her part should have been spelled with a *b* instead of a *w*. Selma was really weird then, always wearing black like Morticia or Elvira, pretending she was using her stupid cat to put spells on people. That cat was so dumb it couldn't have caught a mouse if it danced on his paws."

"The hours we spent painting sets for that play," said Peggy.

"Just so we could keep our eyes on Chuck and Tom." Lavinia laughed, turning the page. "Oh, look at the prom pictures. There we are, you with Tom, me with Chuck, dancing to a slow number. Who's that in the background with Selma?"

Peggy leaned forward to get a better look. "That's Stu McIntyre."

"Stu?" Lavinia looked again. "I forgot he took Selma to the prom that year. I didn't recognize him with all that wild hair."

While Lavinia looked at the annuals, Peggy poked through boxes. Finally she stood up and arched her back to get the kinks out. "The Nancy Drew books must be in the attic."

The grandfather clock in the hall above their heads bonged eleven.

"I wonder if the rain's stopped," said Lavinia.

The moon was beginning to peek through the clouds, the rain reduced to an intermittent drizzle.

"Let's go for a walk. I want some fresh air," said Peggy.

"C'mon. We'll sneak over to Selma's, like we did when we were in high school."

The two women slipped on sneakers and rain ponchos.

Selma's house was two blocks away on Oak Street. A small Georgian-style two-story brick, one of two in Cobb's Landing, originally built by Josiah Cobb as a wedding gift for his daughter, a miniature version of the home he'd built for himself on the other side of Acorn Lane the year his daughter was born. Selma's house sat back from the street on a large corner lot. A boomerang-shaped driveway passed in front of the house, providing access from Oak Street and Acorn Lane, the side street.

"Do you see what I see?" whispered Lavinia as they approached the house. "Isn't that Selma's car parked in front of the house?"

Peggy tugged at Lavinia's arm, motioning to her to stand still. "Look at the second floor," Peggy whispered. "I see a light up there."

"I told you Selma wasn't dead," said Lavinia.

The women stayed in the shadows. "That's not an ordinary light," said Peggy. "It's a flashlight. Someone's up there. I'm going around back to get a better look. You go around the front. Stick to the sidewalk. I'll meet you at the driveway on Acorn Lane."

Peggy pulled her poncho hood over her head and slipped along the L-shaped brick wall separating Selma's house from her neighbors.

As Lavinia turned the corner onto Acorn Lane, she was so intent on looking up at the house that at first she missed seeing a couple heading in her direction. When she caught sight of them, her heart began pounding. She quickly stooped and backed through a gap in the hedge into Selma's front yard, where she watched the couple approach unobserved. That can't be, she thought. It's not possible.

Missy and Ian passed by on the sidewalk. Lavinia stayed put, quiet as a mouse, until the pair turned onto Oak Street and were no longer visible.

Lavinia turned her head to look up at the house. The only light now visible was the reflected moonlight in the second-story windows. The ground-floor windows were shuttered. She scooted along the hedge to the Acorn Lane driveway entrance as Peggy was just approaching from the back of the house. "Let's get out of here fast," she whispered, grabbing Peggy's sleeve. They sprinted all the way back to Peggy's house.

When they were safely inside Peggy's kitchen, Lavinia clung to a chair back for support while she caught her breath.

"Are you all right?" asked Peggy.

Lavinia burst out laughing. "That was incredible! I haven't had so much fun since the night we dropped the beer cans in Selma's trash." She laughed until her stomach hurt. Then said breathlessly, "Did you see them?"

"See who?"

"Missy and Ian."

"Where?"

"They were outside Selma's house."

"Do you think they were inside the house?"

"I don't know."

"What do you think they were doing there?"

"Ripping off the silver. What do I know? Those two are really spooky. They pop out of nowhere when you least expect them." Lavinia headed for the basement stairs. "I'm too wired to sleep. Put on some coffee. I'll be right back."

Lavinia came into the kitchen clutching the high school annuals. While Peggy made the coffee, Lavinia flipped through the pages until she found the pictures of the senior class play. She sat studying the picture of Selma in the black wig she'd worn in the play.

"Check this out, PJ."

"We've already looked at those pictures," said Peggy.

"Look again," said Lavinia. "It helps if you squint a little. Take the book to the window and look at the picture in the moonlight."

Peggy humored her friend.

"Well?"

Peggy shrugged. "What am I supposed to see?"

"Missy."

"What about her?"

"In that black wig Selma looks like Missy. Can't you see the resemblance?"

Peggy looked again. "What made you think of it?"

"When I saw Missy tonight in the moonlight. At first I really freaked out. I thought it was Selma walking with Ian. Talk about your night of the living dead."

Peggy laughed. "You've been watching too many Sci-Fi Channel movies with Charlie."

"Go ahead and laugh, PJ. You can learn a lot by watching old movies."

"Do you think Selma's dead?"

"I'm still not sure. But I'll tell you this. I've been asking around and no one's seen Selma since Tuesday afternoon. Before she was supposed to meet you." Lavinia thought for a minute. "Selma's probably off shacked up somewhere with her latest fling. She'll come back next week looking very pleased with herself and snickering at all of us. It won't be the first time." Lavinia yawned. "I'm beat. Let's call it a night."

When Lavinia was sound asleep in Nicky's room and Peggy had locked up for the night, she sat in her window seat looking again at the pictures of the senior class play.

Seen in moonlight, the younger Selma in the black wig really did bear an uncanny resemblance to Missy. This is too weird, thought Peggy. She vowed she would find out what really happened to Selma. And she knew just where to begin.

CHAPTER 19

"DO I SMELL COFFEE?" LAVINIA HELPED HERSELF TO a cup and sat down at the kitchen table, where Peggy was busy writing notes to herself. "Did you stay up all night?"

"I slept for a couple of hours," Peggy replied. "I couldn't stop thinking about Selma. What do we really know about her?"

"Aside from her being a thorn in our sides forever?"

"I mean about her family. Where she came from. That sort of thing."

"Oh." Lavinia sipped her coffee. "Didn't she move here when we were in sixth grade? Or was it fifth? My brain isn't functioning yet." She glanced at the kitchen wall clock. "It's only seven-thirty and I'm on my first cup of coffee."

"Her parents came here to run the button factory. Selma always bragged that her mother was related to Josiah Cobb."

"They ran it all right. Ran it right into the ground. Then ran off with the pension fund. I'm surprised Selma stuck it out here."

"I don't like her any more than you do, Lovey. But you

can't blame Selma for what her parents did. After all, they left her flat broke, too. Don't you remember the scandal? Her tuition check bounced and she had to leave college. All she had to come back to was the house here in Cobb's Landing. People felt sorry for her."

"That may be true," said Lavinia grudgingly. "But what has she done with her life since then? You and I both work, we've always worked since we were old enough to baby-sit. We had part-time jobs in high school while Selma lolled around. What does Selma do with herself?"

"There was the antique store."

"In this town? The whole town is an antique. No one had any money to buy her overpriced junk. How long did that last?"

"A month or two."

"Seems to me all she's done with her life is chase after anything in pants. She was never happy unless she was making someone else, usually another woman, miserable." Lavinia got up to pour more coffee. "I can't forgive her for that."

"We both know you're talking about her flirtation with Tom. That's all it was. A flirtation. Too much brandy in the Christmas eggnog."

"Uh-huh. And that big old smooch we walked in on? Where there wasn't any mistletoe?"

"Tom and I had a rocky couple of months after that episode, but we'd made up by Valentine's Day. He was making heart-shaped waffles for me the morning he died."

Lavinia reached over to pat her friend's hand. The two women sat silently for a moment, sipping their coffee.

"I found the Nancy Drew books," Peggy said brightly. "They were in a box in the attic. Take a couple home with you."

"You're really serious about this sleuthing thing, aren't you."

"It'll be fun. Like the scavenger hunts we used to have as kids," said Peggy. "Today we're going to the old cemetery."

"What are we going to do there?"

"I want to check out the tombstones. I've got other things on my list, but it's Sunday and every other place is closed."

"Hey, Mom, when are you coming home?" They turned to see Charlie peering through the kitchen screen door. "You promised to make breakfast. We're hungry. You always make waffles on Sunday."

Lavinia turned to Peggy. "Waffles okay with you?"

Peggy smiled. "As long as they're square and you make them in your kitchen, not mine."

Lavinia winked. "I use the ready-made toaster kind. They're quick and easy."

"Come on, Mom. We've got baseball practice at eleven. Nicky and I want to hit a few balls first."

After breakfast Chuck and the boys went off to baseball practice. Peggy and Lavinia took Buster for a walk through town up to the old cemetery. The wrought iron gate in front of the cemetery—where Peggy had parked while waiting for Selma to show—was unlocked, the padlock hanging open on the rusting chain.

This doesn't look nearly as spooky today as it did the other night, Peggy thought. She took a deep breath and walked through the gate. Once inside, she let Buster off his leash.

The old cemetery sat on land that was too poor for farming. It had once been part of a churchyard, but the church itself was long gone. Destroyed by lightning during a freak summer storm.

"What are we looking for up here?" asked Lavinia.

"I want to look at the tombstones for Josiah Cobb and any members of his family, and then I want to check out the pine trees."

"Pine trees? Peggy, are you nuts?"

"Don't you remember? Stu said there were pine needles in the dead woman's clothing."

"There are a million different varieties of pine trees. What type of needles? Long? Short?"

"He didn't say."

"Talk about a needle in a haystack."

Peggy smiled and kept walking.

They walked past stones that were standing, stones that were flat on the ground, stones that were listing. Many were rectangular; some had rounded tops. And some had been cut into a shape that Lavinia said "looked like the head of a ghost with his shoulders hunched." Most of the grave markers were made of local granite; only a few were imported marble.

There were no elaborate mausoleums or statues of angels to protect the dead. The carvings were simple. Many had only first and last names with the dates of birth and death. Scattered throughout the cemetery were the stones with the quaint inscriptions. At the top of one grave marker, a hand pointed to the sky.

"That's what I call an optimist," said Peggy.

The graves of infants and children were particularly touching.

Lavinia commented that there must have been a major influenza epidemic in 1820. "Too many people died that year for it to be a coincidence."

At last they arrived at the gravesite of Josiah Cobb. Born 1735, died 1793. Next to that another stone. Elizabeth Goodwin Cobb, 1743–1789.

"We know they had at least one child, a daughter," said Peggy. "Do you see her grave?"

Lavinia looked at neighboring plots. "Here's Martha Cobb Martin, 1763 to 1820. Was that her name?"

"I'm not sure. I'll write it down and look it up later."

"Next to Martha is John Martin, 1760 to 1820."

"I'll write that one down, too. Let's go check out the pine trees." Peggy whistled to Buster. They headed toward the very top of the cemetery, where a row of pines, serving as a windbreak, rose toward the sky. Peggy reached into her purse and pulled out a handful of small plastic freezer bags and an extra ballpoint pen. She gave Lavinia the pen and a few bags. "Put some pine needles from each type of tree into one of these bags, write on the label where the tree is located. I'll do the same. We'll match them with a plant book when we get home."

They wandered around gathering needles, pinecones, and anything else they thought might be important. Separating the cemetery from the lot formerly occupied by the church was an area of shrublike trees with green needles and reddish bark. A few trees still bore distinctive red berries.

Buster was nosing about the base of one of the trees.

Peggy was no botanical expert, but she did recognize a yew and knew it was poisonous to humans and animals. "Buster, come!" Peggy ran to grab Buster's collar and put him back on the leash. "Lovey, take the dog, will you? There's something I want to look at."

Lavinia held on to Buster while Peggy stooped to get a better look at whatever had attracted Buster's attention.

Using two of the plastic bags as makeshift mittens, Peggy retrieved the booty and bagged it. She sat back on her haunches, staring at the base of the tree. "I wish we'd brought a camera with us."

"PJ, what did you find?"

Peggy held up the plastic bag for Lavinia's inspection. Inside the bag was a gold locket on a broken rope chain. On the locket, engraved in an old-fashioned script, were the initials *SGT*.

CHAPTER 20

"WHY DO YOU WANT A CAMERA?"

"There are marks on that tree trunk. Look at the bark."

"What sort of marks?"

"I'll hold Buster, you go look."

Lavinia looked at the tree, then turned to Peggy. "What do you suppose made those marks? An animal?"

"A human animal," said Peggy. "You stay here at the tree, so we'll know which one it is. I'll take Buster home. I've got some shots left on the disposable camera I bought for the ribbon cutting. You want anything?"

"I really need to pee. Tell you what. I'll take Buster home. Where's the camera?"

"On the front hall table. You know where to find the spare key. Here. Take the stuff I collected." Peggy shoved everything into a plastic grocery bag and handed it to Lavinia.

Peggy kept her vigil at the yew tree while Lavinia trotted down the hill, Buster at her heels. She looked at the marks again. Could the dirt under Selma's nails actually be bark?

Lavinia returned with the camera and a measuring tape.

"If we're going to do this, let's do it right." She extended the tape and held it parallel to the tree trunk while Peggy snapped the last four shots in the camera.

They left the old cemetery to spend the afternoon at the baseball field watching their sons whip the opposition nine to three.

Monday morning Peggy drove Nick and Charlie to school, then headed off to the discount mall thirty miles away to do her shopping and run errands.

First she dropped off the disposable camera for processing.

"Ready Thursday," the clerk said, snapping her gum, eager to get back to reading the latest lurid tabloid.

"That long?"

"I can have them ready for you in an hour, but it'll cost extra."

Peggy hesitated, thinking of the bank loan payments she had to make and the state of her finances. In another month Nicky would need new sneakers. She looked through the envelope she always carried in her purse. Luck was on her side.

"I've got a coupon for one-hour processing and double prints," she said, putting the piece of paper on the counter.

The clerk stapled the coupon to the film envelope. "Come back in an hour."

Peggy finished her biweekly grocery shopping in a little over an hour. Staples like milk and bread she replenished at the general store in Cobb's Landing, but even with the price of gas, it was cheaper to make the round trip to the discount store twice a month for everything else. Peggy stored the frozen food in the large cooler she always kept in the trunk of her car. She'd even remembered to buy frozen waffles as a treat for Nicky. The store brand was on a two-for-one coupon special.

Peggy picked up her pictures and put them in her purse. The next stop was the library at the university extension.

The library was the best place Peggy could imagine

being. Better than shopping. She soon had a pile of books stacked on the table in front of her.

She began reading and making notes. Who knew there was so much to know about yews? She looked over what she'd written.

"The yew is an evergreen tree, leaves are dark green with milky green undersides about one-half to one and one-half inches long. Shiny on the top, matte on the bottom. The yew grows slowly, new trunks generate from the original branches which grow down into the ground to form new stems which then rise up around the old central growth as separate but linked trunks. The reddish-brown bark is about one-eighth inch thick. Some yews in Europe are thought to be four thousand years old. The wood was prized for furniture because of its resistance to insects and fungi. It was also used in the Middle Ages to make long bows for archery.

"The yew is food for elk, deer, moose, and caribou, but toxic to horses and cattle. One mouthful can kill a cow in five minutes. All parts of the plant are toxic, although birds eat the bright red berries—distinguished by a cuplike hole on the top—and spread the seeds in their droppings. Death from yews is caused by an alkaloid that causes cardiac and respiratory collapse. Symptoms of yew poisoning include: nausea and vomiting, increased salivation, stomachache, diarrhea, sleepiness, shortage of breath, trembling, and spasms."

Not very pleasant, thought Peggy. Who would want one of those trees in their yard? She was glad she'd disposed of the plastic bags she'd used as gloves when touching the tree to retrieve the locket.

"Yews were sacred to the Druids, who built their temples near these trees, and the early Christians. Yews are often found in present and former churchyards." Aha! No wonder they're growing next to the old cemetery. Peggy read on.

"Yews were considered protection against evil and

sprigs of yew were often thrown into graves or on top of coffins. Also considered the tree of death and rebirth."

Peggy thumbed through a book of quotations looking for references to yew. What she found made her eyes pop and mouth drop.

> *Scale of dragon, tooth of wolf,*
> *Witch's mummy, maw and gulf*
> *Of the ravined salt-sea shark,*
> *Root of hemlock digged i' th' dark,*
> *Liver of blaspheming Jew,*
> *Gall of goat, and slips of yew*
> *Slivered in the moon's eclipse,*
> *Nose of Turk, and Tartar's lips,*
> *Finger of birth-strangled babe*
> *Ditch-delivered by a drab*
> *Make the gruel thick and slab.*
> *Add thereto a tiger's chaudron*
> *For th' ingredience of our cauldron.*

> —WILLIAM SHAKESPEARE, *Macbeth*
> (Third Witch, Act IV, Scene i)

"*Slips of yew/Slivered in the moon's eclipse*"? Holy crap, as Nicky was fond of saying when he didn't think Peggy could hear him, what on earth was going on in Cobb's Landing? And how was Selma involved? A lunar eclipse on the night of Selma's death was too coincidental for comfort.

Just wait until Lovey hears about this. Peggy checked out an armload of books and ran to her car.

CHAPTER 21

"WHAT IN THE HELL IS GOING ON IN COBB'S LAND-ing?" Lavinia slapped a sheet of paper on the counter at Tom's Tools. "I'm so mad I can barely speak. You've got some nerve, Peggy Jean Turner. You've also got some explaining to do, and it had better be good."

Gulp. That wasn't quite the reaction I was expecting, thought Peggy. "Lovey, what are you talking about?"

"This." Lavinia jabbed at the paper with her finger. "Read it. Now."

Peggy picked up the letter-sized sheet headed COMMIT-TEE FOR COLONIAL VILLAGE, addressed to Mr. and Mrs. Charles Cooper. It read:

> *You are hereby informed that unless your satellite dish is either covered or removed from your property within forty-eight hours, you will be subject to a fine of $50.00 and/or a punishment of three hours in the stocks.*

—PJ Turner, Mayor of Cobb's Landing

Peggy turned pale with shock and rage. "I didn't write this, Lovey. I know absolutely nothing about it. It's not even signed. My name is typed. And that's not how I sign my letters. This is either a very cruel joke or a complete forgery, and I'm going to get to the bottom of it. We're going to see Max."

"Good afternoon, ladies." Max breezed in the door as if he hadn't a care in the world. "Glad to see the weather's cleared up. I've brought you copies of the clippings from the wonderful publicity we got from Saturday's ribbon cutting. We've already had five thousand hits on the Colonial Village website."

"Cut the crap, Max," said Peggy. "You've got some explaining to do." She waved the letter in Max's face.

"Let me see that." Max grabbed the paper from Peggy's hand and read every word. "My, my, my."

"Max, I didn't write that letter. I want to know who did and I want to know right now."

Max turned on his heel and was gone.

"PJ, I didn't really believe you wrote it," said Lavinia. "But the more I read it, the madder I got. When you weren't around this morning, it looked like you were hiding."

"Hiding? I went shopping. And then to the library. I told you yesterday what I was going to do."

"I forgot. I was so mad. I'm not the only one who got a letter. Everyone in this town who has a dish or TV antenna received one." Lavinia began to giggle. "You'll probably find one in your own letter box."

Max returned a few minutes later with Missy. "Missy, you will apologize immediately to Mrs. Cooper and especially to Mayor Turner. Forgery is a crime."

"Max, I still think it's a good idea," said Missy. "You wanted the stocks installed to amuse the tourists; why can't we put them to practical use? Those satellite dishes have got to go."

"Missy, I've lost my patience with you," said Max. "Go

clean out your office and pack your bags. I'm sending you back to the regional office."

"Oh no, Max," said Missy. "Please don't send me back there."

"Go," said Max. "Go before I really lose my temper." Max turned beet red from head to toe, looking as if he was about to succumb to heat stroke.

Missy went.

"You look all hot and bothered, Max. Can I get you a glass of water?" asked Peggy.

"Water?" Max made a face, the way Nicky did when Peggy tried to give him a dose of cod liver oil in the winter. "I never touch the stuff." Max shuddered.

"Just where *is* the regional office, Max?" Peggy asked sweetly.

"Providence," Max snapped. For the first time since his arrival in Cobb's Landing, Max appeared completely discombobulated. He quickly recovered his composure. "My deepest apologies, Mayor Turner, Mrs. Cooper. I will make amends, I promise you."

"You could tear up those loan papers I signed," Peggy said.

Max hesitated for a fraction of a second. "Very well, consider it done," he said, looking as if he'd just sucked on a very sour lemon. "Stop by my office at the bank first thing tomorrow morning."

With a distracted wave, Max was gone. The screen door slammed shut behind him.

Lavinia looked at the door, still quivering on its hinges, then at Peggy. "What just happened here, PJ?"

"Damned if I know, Lovey. But I think I just got out of hock. Let's go to my house. I've got lots to tell you."

Later that afternoon, a public apology to all residents of Cobb's Landing, acknowledging the satellite dish letter was a complete fake and entirely the work of a disgruntled staff member at the bank, appeared on the community message board in the town square. The apology was signed by Max, in red ink.

CHAPTER 22

"GUESS WHO I SAW AT THE BUS STOP THIS AFTER-noon, Mom?" Nicky reached for another cookie to go with his after-school glass of milk.

"Who, dear?" Peggy was still feeling a little light-headed. Being suddenly debt-free was quite a shock. Max had better keep his promise, Peggy thought. But I've got Lovey as a witness. Let's see, the bank opens at nine. I'll be there at nine on the dot.

"Max. He was putting Missy on the bus for Boston. She didn't look very happy."

"That's nice, dear." Peggy stood up and kissed the top of her son's head. "I feel a little woozy. I'm going to take a nap. Wake me in an hour. Go do your homework so we can watch a movie together after supper. I put a surprise in the freezer for you."

The next morning Peggy was at the bank at nine sharp.

"Mayor Turner, how nice to see you again." Ian cupped Peggy's elbow with his palm, guiding her toward his of-fice. "Max had some out-of-town business to take care of, but he told me you were coming in this morning and asked me to fill in for him."

"Max goes out of town a lot," said Peggy. "Where exactly does he go?"

Ian smiled. Those teeth are so white they must glow in the dark, thought Peggy. "Max has a lot of irons in the fire," he replied.

"In Providence?" said Peggy.

"And other places." Ian handed Peggy a large manila envelope. "I think you'll find everything is in order."

"If you don't mind, I'll take a look." Peggy opened the envelope. Max had kept his word. The promissory notes she signed were all stamped CANCELED. The overdraft account was marked PAID IN FULL. She glanced at the bottom lines on the bank statements for her personal checking and the Tom's Tools accounts. She was solvent again. Barely. But she wouldn't have to worry about how she was going to pay for Nicky's new sneakers. She tucked the envelope under her arm and rose to leave Ian's office.

"Have you got time for a cup of coffee?" asked Ian, cranking up the charm level, as he walked with Peggy to the front door of the bank. "We've never had a chance to talk. I really could use your advice."

They strolled up Main Street to Clemmie's Café. As they passed the space that had once been billed as Selma's Tart Shoppe, then Missy's Muffin Shoppe, a new sign was being hung: IAN'S BOOKE NOOKE. Inside workmen were busy removing pastry cases and installing floor-to-ceiling shelves. Peggy turned to look at Ian.

"That's what I wanted to talk to you about," said Ian as they entered Clemmie's. "I hear you're a real bookworm." Another warm smile. "Would you like a muffin with your coffee?"

Clemmie's Café was packed with Cobb's Landing residents, enjoying the novelty of having the café open again. Most would spend the morning nursing one cup of coffee until the free refills ended at ten-thirty before the lunch trade started. Ian grabbed the last table for two.

While they waited for their order, Peggy said, "How did you know I liked books?"

"Max told me. He makes it his business to know everything about . . ." Ian paused, choosing his next words carefully. ". . . the people he's interested in. He thought you
might give me a hand selecting stock for the new shop."

"I'm really busy at the hardware store."

Ian slid his hand over Peggy's and looked into her eyes.
His hand felt warm on top of hers. "Please? It would mean
a lot to me."

Against her better judgment, Peggy agreed.

"I'll bring the catalogs to the hardware store. I need to
get some book orders placed this afternoon if I'm going to
be open this weekend. Did Max tell you? We've already
had over five thousand hits on the website."

"Don't you find that a little incongruous?" asked Peggy.

"What?" Ian looked puzzled.

"Using an Internet website to promote Colonial Village?"

Ian shrugged. "As Ralph Waldo Emerson said, 'A fool-
ish consistency . . .'"

Peggy chimed in. ". . . is the hobgoblin of little
minds.'" They finished the quote together and laughed.
Peggy felt very clever and smart. "I've always wanted to
go to Walden Pond," she said.

"I've been there," said Ian. "It's not much now. Not like
it was when Thoreau built his cabin. I could take you there
sometime if you'd like."

Ian and Peggy spent the rest of the morning together at
the hardware store poring over book catalogs. Peggy was
in her element.

"We've covered the adult selections. Now about the
children's books," said Ian, putting more catalogs on the
counter. "What does your son like to read? He's ten?"

Peggy nodded.

Ian checked his watch. "I've got to fax these orders.
Why don't you take the catalogs home, get your son's
input, and I'll stop by for them later. Shall we say eight
o'clock?"

Later that afternoon Lavinia came into the store.

"What's this I hear about you and Ian at Clemmie's this morning?"

"He asked me to help him place orders for the new book shop."

"I saw the new sign. I didn't think Ian was really the book type. I would have pegged him for a model on the cover of a men's fashion magazine. No one in Cobb's Landing dresses that well."

"He quoted Emerson to me this morning."

"Uh-huh," said Lavinia with a smile. "That's not the way I heard it."

"What did you hear?"

"That you two were real cozy. That you were practically holding hands over coffee. The whole town is buzzing about it. You want to come over tonight? I stopped at the county courthouse this afternoon on my way home from the hospital."

"I can't."

"Why not?"

"Ian is coming over at eight to pick up the last of the book catalogs."

"Uh-huh." Lavinia flashed Peggy another smile. "Your honor, I rest my case." She chuckled to herself as she left the hardware store.

CHAPTER 23

BY SEVEN-THIRTY PEGGY HAD CLEANED UP THE kitchen, run a dust cloth over the living room furniture, sent Nicky up to his room to do his homework, changed clothes, splashed on a little cologne from the bottle Lovey had given her for Christmas, and was feeling as fluttery as Laura Wingfield waiting for a gentleman caller.

You're a grown woman, Peggy Turner, she muttered to herself, you have a son, you run a business, you have responsibilities. Stop acting like a silly schoolgirl. But her heart kept thumping at an accelerated pace. Eight years *was* a long time.

The grandfather clock hadn't yet chimed eight when there was a knock on the front door. To anyone else Peggy would have yelled "Come on in" or "Door's open" and continued what she was doing. But not tonight. She went to the screen door and opened it. There stood Stu McIntyre.

"Hi, Peggy, I saw your light on. I tried catching you at the hardware store this afternoon, but you must have closed up early. I finally got the medical examiner's report.

Can I come in?" He glanced at the living room. "You expecting company?"

Peggy dodged Stu's question with one of her own. "Would you like a cup of coffee?"

They headed back to the kitchen, where Peggy poured a cup from the pot she'd just made.

Stu was pulling the medical examiner's report from his shirt pocket when Nicky called down from upstairs.

"Mom, there's someone at the front door. Want me to get it?"

"I'll go," Peggy called back to her son.

There stood Ian with a long, narrow brown paper bag cradled in the crook of his left arm. He smells better than I do, Peggy thought, inhaling the spicy scent of his aftershave.

As Peggy opened the door to let Ian in, Stu approached from the kitchen.

"If I've come at a bad time," Ian said.

"Peggy and I were just going over some town business," said Stu, leaning against the kitchen doorjamb.

"I see." Ian handed the paper bag to Peggy. "I'll leave you with this then. You might want to put it in the refrigerator."

"Wait, Ian." Peggy scooped up the book catalogs from the coffee table. "I've put sticky notes on some of the pages."

"I'll look them over tonight. Good night, Peggy. And thanks for all your trouble. I'll let myself out."

Peggy peeked into the paper bag as she went back into the kitchen. Inside was a bottle of white wine that cost more than anything she'd ever been able to afford. She stored the bottle on its side in the refrigerator, then poured herself a cup of coffee.

"About that medical report," she said brightly.

"The dental records confirmed the body is Selma Thomas," said Stu. "The medical examiner thinks she died of heart failure. He's released the body to the undertaker. The funeral is Saturday morning at ten."

"Was the dirt under her fingernails tested?"

"I don't know. Why?"

Peggy went to get the photo envelope from her purse. "Lovey and I took Buster for a walk in the old cemetery Sunday afternoon before the baseball game. We found this caught in the trunk of a yew tree near the old church." She got out the plastic bag containing the locket. "Look at the initials. *SGT.*"

Stu swallowed hard. "I gave Selma that locket for her birthday when we were in high school."

"I know you took her to the senior prom."

Stu looked at Peggy. "How did you remember that?"

"Lovey and I were looking at our old annuals last weekend."

Stu turned the plastic bag over and over in his hands. "I can't believe she kept it all these years."

"Was it serious with you and Selma?" Peggy asked.

"She thought so. She thought this locket meant we were sort of engaged to be engaged. Whatever that meant. She wanted my senior class ring, but I told her I wasn't ready to go steady."

"What happened?"

"We hung around together the summer after graduation, then she went away to that fancy girls' college. It wasn't the same for us when she came home for Christmas vacation."

Peggy read Stu some of the notes she'd taken on yews. Then she showed him the photos of the scratches in the tree bark.

"Can I keep these pictures?"

"Sure. I got double prints." Peggy handed the dupes to Stu.

"Do you think the bark was enough to kill her?" he asked.

"I'm no expert," said Peggy. "I think it would take more than that, don't you? You told me there were pine needles found in her clothing. Did you ever find out what species they were?"

"Good question. I'll ask the medical examiner." Stu looked at his watch. "I hate to run, Peggy, but I promised to meet Virginia. Thanks for the coffee." Stu let himself out the front door.

Peggy washed out the coffee cups and put them in the dish drainer to dry. She turned out the front light, locked the door, and curled up to watch television with Nicky.

"Gee, Mom," Nicky said, "you sure smell good."

CHAPTER 24

PEGGY WAS HEADING UPSTAIRS TO BED AFTER watching the late news when there was a knock at her kitchen door.

Lavinia stood there with a grin on her face. "I've come to hear all about the big date."

"When Ian arrived, Stu was here. Ian stayed for less than five minutes and left."

"Ian just walked off? I can't say I'm impressed with his persistence."

"We didn't really have a date, Lovey. He was only coming over to pick up the book catalogs. He was just as surprised to see Stu here as I was."

"Tell me what Stu said."

"The body has been positively identified as Selma Thomas. Stu said the funeral will be Saturday morning at ten."

Lavinia was silent for a moment. "I'm sorry. Selma was a real pain, but she didn't deserve to die that young. What killed her?"

"No one is sure. I told Stu that I thought the dirt under

her fingernails might be bark from the yew tree. He's going to tell the medical examiner."

"Good thinking, PJ."

"That's what I wanted to tell you about yesterday, but you were in such a lather about the satellite dish letter."

"I really went off the deep end, didn't I? I always wanted to be a drama queen. Tell me what you found out about yews." Lavinia grinned. "I don't believe I said that with a straight face."

"They're highly poisonous to some animals and to humans. Shakespeare wrote about them in *Macbeth*. About one of the three witches gathering yew leaves during the moon's eclipse."

"Whew. That's really creepy. Sounds like Selma was carrying her witch act a little too far and it backfired on her."

"I also showed Stu the locket we found in the cemetery. Guess what? Stu gave that locket to Selma when we all were in high school."

"Really? And she kept it all these years? She must have been wearing it the night she died. Was it only a week ago?" Lavinia thought for a moment. "I don't remember Stu and Selma being that serious."

"I didn't either. Stu said she was more serious about the relationship than he was. She regarded them as engaged to be engaged."

"Whatever that means," said Lavinia. "I'll have to ask Chuck about Stu and Selma. He has a better memory for ancient history than I do."

"What were you doing at the county courthouse?"

"Oh that," said Lavinia. "I'll go get the paper. This is really interesting." Lavinia scampered out Peggy's kitchen door, through the fence gate, and into her own kitchen. She was back before Peggy had finished putting Nicky's breakfast dishes on the table.

"Selma's parents were totally self-centered creeps," said Lavinia. "Not only did they screw the town when they scampered off to South America—or wherever it was they went—with the button factory pension fund, but they gave Selma the shaft as well. Look at this." She handed Peggy a photocopy.

"What is it?"

"It's a copy of the land records for Selma's house. Her parents put the house into a trust. All Selma got was a life interest."

"So when Selma died . . ."

"Right. That was the end of it. The house wasn't hers to sell or leave to anyone. She got kicked out of college, came home to find her parents gone, and all they left her was a place to live until she died. She couldn't even mortgage it."

"That's sad," said Peggy. "Remember how we used to envy Selma because she had all the pretty new party dresses?"

"She was such a brat about those dresses. Showing off to all the other kids and the teachers like she was a little princess."

"True. She was a brat. But we always knew our parents loved us. I'd rather have that memory than a party dress."

Lavinia's eyes began to mist.

"Lovey, if Selma couldn't use the house to raise cash, what did she live on all these years?"

"Beats me."

"We're going to find out. I'll meet you out front in five minutes."

"Now? It's after eleven."

"It has to be now. We'll never get another chance when everyone finds out that Selma is really dead. We'll be home in fifteen minutes."

Peggy and Lavinia slipped over to Selma's house. The car was still parked in front as it had been a few nights earlier. All the windows were dark.

"How are we going to get inside?" whispered Lavinia.

"We'll go around the back, there's probably a spare key there."

Peggy found the spare key hidden in a flower pot next

to the back door. Alarm systems were unknown in a town where everyone trusted their neighbors.

They entered the kitchen.

Peggy put her thumb on the switch of the small disposable flashlight, a gift from Nicky in her Christmas stocking, that she kept on her key ring. The green light didn't have much power, but it was enough to see by.

Except for the hum of the refrigerator, the kitchen was quiet. "Don't open the refrigerator," said Peggy. "We don't want anyone to see the light."

The kitchen counters were wiped clean. A single cup rested in the dish drainer. Paper plates were stacked next to a microwave oven.

They crept through the pantry into the dining room. Then into the parlor, the living room, and the library. A mahogany staircase led to the second floor.

Peggy started up the stairs, but Lavinia held her back. "I think someone's watching us."

"Don't be silly, Lovey. The house is empty. Three more minutes and we're out of here."

A quick tour of the upstairs and they were back at the staircase.

"I *know* someone's watching us," said Lavinia.

"We're going home," said Peggy, pointing her light down the staircase.

A pair of disembodied eyes glowed at the foot of the stairs.

Lavinia clutched Peggy's arm. "I'm not going down those stairs."

"We can't stay here all night."

The eyes began moving toward them.

Lavinia's hands felt clammy on Peggy's arm.

The eyes got closer, then stopped.

Peggy leaned down to stroke the black cat rubbing against her leg.

"Now what are we going to do?" whispered Lavinia.

"We're getting out of here," said Peggy.

Five minutes later they were at Lavinia's front door.

Chuck stood in the doorway in his bare feet, wearing only a T-shirt and briefs. His hair was rumpled, his arms were crossed, and there was a scowl on his normally pleasant face. "Where in the hell have you been?" he said to his wife.

CHAPTER 25

"LOWER YOUR VOICE, CHUCK, DO YOU WANT TO wake the entire neighborhood?" Lavinia marched through the house into her kitchen, Chuck and Peggy on her heels. "Coffee? Or something stronger? Chuck, get out your bottle of Seagram's. I need a drink."

"Will someone tell me what's going on?" said Chuck.

Lavinia and Peggy exchanged glances.

"We might as well tell him," said Peggy.

Interrupting each other frequently, the story finally came out.

"Make me one, too, honey," Chuck said as Lavinia got up to freshen her drink. "PJ, you want a topper on that?"

Peggy shook her head. She poured more 7-Up into her already-watered-down drink.

"The house was empty?" asked Chuck.

"Stripped to the walls," said Lavinia.

"Except for a cheap bed and dresser upstairs, a card table and chairs in the dining room, a ratty old lounger and small television in the library," said Peggy. "Selma must have sold everything else. You could see the spots on the walls where pictures used to hang."

"The only books left in the library were used paper-backs," said Lavinia.

"We have to do something about the cat," said Peggy.

"What cat?" asked Chuck.

Lavinia told that part of the story, omitting her fear and sweating palms. Peggy's lips twitched, but she kept quiet.

"You left the cat in the house?" said Chuck.

"Honey, what could we do? If we took it with us, some-one would know we'd been there," said Lavinia. "We didn't have time to look for cat food."

"I wanted to put it outside," said Peggy. "But it may have been strictly an indoor cat. It wasn't wearing a collar. I'm worried about it. Who knows when it last had anything to eat or drink."

"You have to tell Stu," said Chuck. "Someone may have seen you two. Not everyone keeps farmer's hours in Cobb's Landing." Chuck got up and went to the phone to dial Stu's number.

"It's one in the morning," said Lavinia. "Can't this wait until after dawn?"

"He may not be home," said Peggy. "He said he was going to meet Virginia."

Chuck hung up the phone.

"They've become quite an item," said Lavinia. "Honey, what do you remember about Stu and Selma?"

"Didn't they go out for a while in high school?" said Chuck.

"He took her to the senior prom," said Lavinia.

"Stu said they hung out together the summer after grad-uation," said Peggy.

"It's too late to talk about this now," said Chuck. "I'm going back to bed. PJ, call Stu first thing in the morning. If you don't, I will."

CHAPTER 26

WHEN NICKY WAS SAFELY OFF TO SCHOOL, PEGGY
dialed Stu's number. He answered on the first ring. He arrived at Peggy's house half an hour later. He'd showered
and shaved, but was wearing the same white shirt and
khaki slacks he'd worn the night before.

"Is that coffee fresh or from last night?" he asked.

"It's fresh. Help yourself while I call Lovey and
Chuck."

The four adults sat at Peggy's kitchen table. Once again
Peggy and Lavinia told the story of their walk the night before.

"You know I could have you both arrested for breaking
and entering," Stu said.

Peggy glowered at Stu. "We used a key."

"You still were trespassing," Stu replied.

"Can we skip the technicalities," said Lavinia. "We're
worried about the cat."

"Pie."

"What?" said Chuck. "Who said anything about food?"

"Pie," Stu repeated. "Selma's cats were always black

and she named them all Pie. You know, after the cat in the senior class play. I didn't know she still had a cat."

Peggy got up to clear the table and put away the loaf of bread Nicky had left out when he'd made toast for his breakfast. When she couldn't find the twist tie, she tore off a piece of tape from the dispenser she kept on the counter. As she returned to the table, she stumbled and put her hand on Stu's shoulder for support.

Stu looked up at Peggy. "You okay?"

"Fine. It's nothing. I tripped." She smoothed the wrinkle she'd made in the yoke of Stu's shirt.

"Let's go rescue that cat," said Chuck. "I've got to get to school. I've got year-end projects to grade."

The back door key was still in the flowerpot. "I'll take that to the police station for safekeeping," said Stu, pocketing the key.

When they walked into the former dining room, Chuck let out a low whistle. "You weren't kidding, Lovey. This place is bare to the walls. I haven't been in this house since high school, the cast party after the senior play. Then this house looked like a museum. Some of the stuff in here Selma's mother said once belonged to Cobb's daughter. You couldn't turn around without bumping into something. Selma's parents weren't too crazy about having a bunch of teenagers in the house. They were afraid we might break something valuable."

Peggy opened the plastic container of leftover tuna salad she'd brought from her refrigerator. "Here, Pie," she called softly.

The little black cat made a beeline from its hiding place, right for Stu.

"Cats always go for the ones who don't like them," he said, backing away quickly.

Peggy picked up the starving cat and took it into the kitchen. She put the tuna salad on a paper plate and stood watching it eat.

"Who's taking this cat home with them?" Peggy asked. "We can't leave it here."

"I don't like cats and Virginia is allergic to them. Her throat closes up and she can't breathe," said Stu.

"We have two dogs," said Lavinia, "and Charlie has tropical fish."

All eyes were focused on Peggy. "I'll take the cat," she said, wondering how Buster would react. She could always keep the cat at the hardware store to catch mice. She locked the cat in her car and went back into the house.

Chuck left for school, while Lavinia headed off to the hospital. Peggy joined Stu on the second floor, where he was checking to make sure all the windows were securely closed and latched. She noticed that Selma's bed was neatly made, except for a dent in the coverlet where the cat had obviously been sleeping.

"Stu, did you know Selma had been selling off the furniture?"

Stu hesitated before replying. "I knew she got a raw deal when her parents skipped town. But we weren't real close after that." He looked at his watch. "Isn't it time you were opening up the hardware store? I've got to go meet with the medical examiner about that yew bark theory you came up with. He thinks you might be on to something."

CHAPTER 27

"I THOUGHT I WAS THE ONLY ONE WHO KEPT banker's hours." Ian stood next to Peggy's car while she gathered the things she was taking into Tom's Tools. "May I help you with something?"

Peggy scooped up the cat from the backseat. "Hold the cat, will you?"

Pie hissed and spit at Ian, wriggling to get away from him. Tiny claws dug into Peggy's arm.

"Stay here," Peggy said. "I'll put the cat in the storeroom."

When the cat was safely locked inside Tom's Tools, Peggy went back to her car.

"You want to do something about those scratches," said Ian, holding Peggy's wrist while he looked at her arm. "They could get infected. Where's your first aid kit?"

"I always keep one at the checkout counter," said Peggy. "Some people aren't real handy around sharp objects like saws and screwdrivers."

Ian gently cleaned Peggy's scratches with peroxide. "I don't know why that cat doesn't like me," he said. "I generally get along quite well with felines. Have you had it long?"

"No, I'm keeping it for a friend."

"I was wondering if you might be free tonight," said Ian. "I'm expecting some shipments by express mail this afternoon and thought we might have dinner after they're unpacked. I could use your help organizing my window displays."

"I promised Nicky I'd be at his baseball game," said Peggy. "It's the first evening game of the season."

"It appears we've reached an impasse. Another time perhaps." Several women stopped to gawk as Ian sauntered from Tom's Tools across Main Street to the Booke Nooke.

Peggy went into the storeroom to check on the cat. Pie was curled on a top shelf, tail tucked between its front paws, sound asleep. Peggy ran down to the general store, returning with cat food and litter. She put out a bowl of water, then quietly closed the storeroom door. I'll decide later if it's going home with me, she thought.

Business was once again picking up at Tom's Tools. Peggy put away the coffeepot—there was no sense taking sales away from a fellow merchant; though if Clemmie's Café began giving away screws and nails, she'd rethink her decision—but no one seemed to mind. What they really wanted to do was talk and speculate. And talk about the official opening of Colonial Village that weekend.

"When do we start wearing our costumes?"

"Has anyone seen Missy? I heard she left town."

"Do we have to wear costumes to the baseball games?"

Lavinia called from the hospital early that afternoon. "Do me a favor? I'm going to be stuck here until six."

"Don't worry, I'll feed Chuck and Charlie. See you at the ball field."

While she stirred a pan of makings for sloppy joes, and Pie played with a ball of string under the kitchen table, Peggy thought long and hard about something that had been bothering her all day. How could she possibly keep someone on the town payroll who was lying to her?

Lavinia and Chuck invited everyone back to their house after the game to celebrate the Cobb's Landing Patriots eight-to-four win. Charlie and Nicky were the heroes of the game and happy to have a night without homework. They grabbed sodas and popcorn, then went up to Charlie's room to play computer games.

When the grown-ups were hoisting their second beer, Virginia stood up and put her arm around Stu. "We have an announcement to make," she said as she beamed and held up her left hand, where a tiny diamond sparkled on her ring finger. "We're getting married in July."

"I told you, you should have grabbed him," said Lavinia later that evening when she and Peggy were cleaning up the empties in the backyard and the mess in the kitchen. "That man was ripe for marriage. It could have been you standing there tonight, PJ." She bundled the trash to haul outside. "Stu and Virginia. It seems sudden, but they're both adults. They know what they're doing." She sighed. "A summer wedding. I love summer weddings. Those pretty summer dresses." She turned to Peggy. "We won't have to wear those awful pilgrim costumes to the wedding, will we?"

"What do I know?" said Peggy. "I don't make the rules."

"You're the mayor."

"All right. I hereby declare"—Peggy took a final swig of her beer, then held the empty bottle aloft—"there will be no costumes worn at the wedding."

As Peggy went to sleep, with Pie sprawled across the end of her bed, she wondered why she hadn't shared her suspicions about Stu with Lovey. Because they would sound like sour grapes after the wedding announcement? She knew Stu was lying about the cat. Those were cat hairs on his shirt this morning. From the same cat who was now shedding on her bed. And Peggy could prove it.

CHAPTER 28

BY THURSDAY MORNING, EVERYONE IN COBB'S Landing knew about Stu and Virginia's engagement. At eleven, the bride-to-be made an appearance at Tom's Tools.

"Hi, Virginia," said Peggy, "playing hooky?"

"It's my lunch hour." Virginia handed Peggy a sealed envelope. "I wanted to bring you an invitation."

"A wedding invitation? So soon?"

"No, it's for a picnic Stu and I are having on Memorial Day. It starts at six, after the village is closed. I hope you and Nick can come. It's an engagement party." Virginia reached up to finger the gold locket hanging on a rope chain around her neck.

"That's a beautiful locket," said Peggy.

"Stu gave it to me about a month ago, a preengagement present."

Peggy leaned over the checkout counter to get a closer look. The locket was engraved in an old-fashioned script with three initials: *VGM*.

"What does the *G* stand for?"

"Glover," replied Virginia. "It's a family name." Virginia handed Peggy a second envelope. "Would you mind giving this to the Coopers? I have to get back to school."

After Virginia left Tom's Tools, Peggy felt something rubbing against her ankle. She looked down to see Pie playing at her feet. Virginia's no more allergic to cats than I am, thought Peggy.

"Good morning, Mayor," said Max. "What's this I hear about a wedding?" Without waiting for a response, he continued, "The tourists will love seeing a colonial wedding. Too bad it's not this weekend, most people think funerals are bad for business, not that I agree, but the wedding will be a wonderful attraction for the Fourth of July. We could have the ceremony on the town square. I'll post an announcement on the website."

"Max, you're getting ahead of yourself," said Peggy. "Stu and Virginia might have other plans."

"They work for the town," said Max. "I'm sure you could talk them into it."

"I have no intention of talking them into anything," said Peggy. "It's their wedding and none of the town's business."

"Very well, I'll have a word with them," Max replied. "Tonight, after the town meeting at five. We've got a big weekend ahead of us. The hotel is completely sold out until Tuesday. Our first guests will be arriving tomorrow morning. I can hear the cash registers ringing now. You don't suppose you could postpone that funeral until next week?"

"I didn't make the arrangements," said Peggy.

"Hi, Max," said Lavinia as she breezed in with a bag of sandwiches. She looked at Max's white linen suit. "You're wearing white before Memorial Day? Isn't that rushing the season?"

"Not where I come from," said Max, straightening his red silk bow tie. With a jaunty wave, Max was gone.

"What's Max got up his sleeve today?" asked Lavinia, handing Peggy a ham and swiss on rye. She pulled a backless stool up to the customer side of the counter and began eating her own sandwich.

"Stu and Virginia's wedding. He wanted to make it a tourist event for the Fourth of July. He also wants to postpone Selma's funeral until next week. Says it's bad for business."

"Max has a cash register where his heart should be. I'll be glad when that funeral is over. I'm sure Virginia will have something to say about the wedding."

Peggy handed Lavinia the envelope. "Virginia asked me to give this to you."

"A wedding invitation? So soon?"

Peggy laughed. "That's exactly what I said. No, it's an engagement party on Memorial Day. A picnic after the village closes."

"Oh, geez, we have to wear those costumes on a holiday? It's bad enough we have to wear them for our Sunday afternoon shift at the museum. I've got Monday off at the hospital. I was hoping I wouldn't have to wear a uniform that day. Are you going to open the hardware store?"

"I hadn't really thought about it," said Peggy. "I usually close the store on holidays so I can spend time with Nicky."

"Do it. We'll hide out in your backyard in our swimsuits and work on our tans. That's what we used to do when we were kids."

"Then we'd go down to the river for the first swim of the summer."

"Before we went home, we'd stop at the general store and split a Popsicle," said Lavinia. "We both liked cherry best. Remember how Chuck and Tom would be waiting on their bicycles to chase us home? But Stu was always there to protect us. Even then Stu acted like a cop."

"Lovey, I'm concerned about Stu."

"Why?"

"He's telling stupid lies. Remember yesterday at Selma's house what he said about the cat?"

"Only that he didn't like them."

"He also said Virginia was allergic to cats. Pie was under the counter this morning when Virginia dropped off the picnic invitation."

"What happened? Did she start gasping?" Lavinia grabbed her throat and began making gagging noises.

"That's just it, Lovey. Nothing happened. There's more. Stu had cat hair on his shirt yesterday morning when he was sitting with you and Chuck at my kitchen table."

"He did? How do you know?"

"I picked it off with a piece of tape."

Lavinia's eyes widened. "Well, give you the Nancy Drew award. I was sitting right there and never noticed. Why did you do it?"

"Because he'd just finished telling us that Selma always had black cats named Pie, but he didn't know if she still had a cat. That's when I noticed the cat hair on his shirt. Remember the night before when Ian was coming over to pick up the book catalogs and Stu showed up first?"

"What about it?"

"Stu was dressed in the same clothes he was wearing yesterday morning, the white shirt and khaki pants. He had a date with Virginia that night. The shirt was clean when he came to my house."

"Maybe Virginia has a cat."

"Why would he say later that she was allergic to them? If he'd lie about something as trivial as a cat allergy, what else would he lie about?"

"I don't know, PJ, it's all too confusing. Why don't you stop playing cat-and-mouse games and tell me what you're thinking."

Peggy took a deep breath. "I think Stu was in Selma's house that night."

"What would he be doing there? He already knew Selma was dead."

"That's my point. He knew she wouldn't be around. I think he was looking for something."

"PJ, do you suppose he was there when we were? I told you I thought someone was looking at us."

"How would he have gotten in? We found the spare key in the flower pot."

"He could have used it to unlock the door, then put it right back where he found it. Where is that key now?"

"He took it from me yesterday morning when we went to rescue the cat."

"We'll just have to find another way to get back inside that house," said Lavinia.

CHAPTER 29

THE TOWN MEETING WAS ALMOST OVER WHEN
Lavinia, still in her nurse's uniform, her face flushed, slid
into her seat on the stage next to Peggy. She blew kisses to
Chuck and Charlie; then waggled her fingers at Stu and
Virginia, sitting side by side in the front row of the school
auditorium. "Good thing there are armrests on those
seats," Lavinia muttered to Peggy under her breath. "She's
practically in his lap."

Peggy stifled a giggle.

"Did I miss anything?" asked Lavinia.

"Max put on a great pregame pep rally," Peggy replied.
"I'll tell you about it later. Change your clothes, then come
over for dinner. I've got a big pan of lasagna baking in the
oven. I've invited Stu and Virginia. A last supper before
the village opens."

"Stu and Virginia are coming? Too bad."

"Why?"

"I've got lots to tell you. It'll keep for later."

After one last reminder from Max that as of eight
o'clock Friday morning cars were to be off the streets until
six at night and everyone was required to be in costume for

the flag raising on the town square at nine, the meeting was over.

Ian approached Peggy in the parking lot. "Is it too late to ask you to dinner?"

"I've already invited people to my house." Peggy hesitated, mentally counting her forks and plates. "Why don't you join us? We're having a simple supper in the backyard. Come over in an hour."

Peggy checked the oven to make sure the lasagna was still browning nicely and not dried out or burned, then ran upstairs to change clothes. Before going back to the kitchen, Peggy lured Pie into the bedroom with a kitty treat then closed the door.

"Nicky," she called over her shoulder as she headed down the stairs, "I need your help. On the double."

"Coming, Mom."

Peggy counted on her fingers. Five adults—no, make that six adults—two children. A tight fit at the picnic table, but they'd manage. There'd be more room at the table if she put out the food in the kitchen and everyone helped themselves. She'd sit on one end, Ian at the other; Virginia and Stu on one side with Nicky, the Coopers across from them. The boys wouldn't stay around long, then the adults could spread out and be more comfortable.

"Nicky!"

"Coming, Mom."

Nicky came into the kitchen wearing jeans and a T-shirt.

"Tuck your shirt into your pants, then take these two chairs outside," Peggy said, pointing to two pressed-back wooden kitchen chairs she'd moved to the back door. She handed Nicky a damp cloth. "First, wipe off the picnic table." Where was her tablecloth? The red-and-white-checked one she used outside in the summer. She pawed through a drawer. Found it. Were there enough napkins? She counted quickly. Eight. She put them on the round oak kitchen table along with the silverware and plates.

"Now what, Mom?"

"Set the table for me. Remember, the forks go on the left."

When the loaves of garlic bread were wrapped in foil ready to warm in the oven, Peggy began tearing at a head of lettuce to make a salad.

"Need some help?" Lavinia poked her head in the kitchen door. "Sure smells good in here."

"Stu and Virginia are bringing wine for dinner. Have you got two wineglasses? I only have four."

"Two?"

"I invited Ian to join us."

Lavinia grinned. "Be right back." She reappeared with a glass in each hand. "Where do you want them?"

"Mom! There's someone at the front door."

"Let them in, Nicky."

Stu and Virginia walked into the kitchen bearing raffia-wrapped bottles of Chianti. Ian followed on their heels.

It was dark when the party finished eating dinner. Overhead the Big and Little Dippers appeared in the night sky. Peggy went inside to find candles, to put on the picnic table. As she was lighting the candles, she looked at the trees along the rear fence line. Tiny lights twinkled in the branches.

"Nicky, do you see what I see?"

"Fireflies! C'mon, Charlie. Let's catch some for science class."

"There are jars under the kitchen sink," said Peggy as the boys raced into the house.

While the adults sat drinking their wine, the boys ran around the yard trying to trap fireflies in Mason jars. They soon grew tired of their game and came back to the table.

"Do you remember what makes them glow?" asked Virginia.

"Yeah," said Charlie. "They got two chemicals in their stomachs."

"The chemicals are named after Lucifer," said Nicky.

"And some of the fireflies eat each other," said Charlie.

The boys went inside to do their homework. Stu poured the last of the wine into everyone's glasses.

Ian turned to Virginia. "That's a very pretty pendant you're wearing. May I see it?"

Virginia unhooked the clasp at the back of her neck and handed the chain to Ian. He examined the locket in the candlelight.

"What does the *G* stand for?"

"Glover. It's a family name."

"You're not from Cobb's Landing, are you?"

"No," said Virginia. "I grew up in Massachusetts."

"Really?" said Ian. "Where?"

"A town north of Boston."

"I've spent some time in that area," he replied with an engaging smile. "Which town?"

"Salem," said Virginia. "My family emigrated there from Ireland."

"How interesting," said Ian. "No wonder you recognized the stocks and the dunking stool. I told Max I didn't think those were a good idea. But it's hard to argue with the boss."

Peggy felt a gentle nip on her ankle. Pie leaped onto the picnic table and sat, tail curled around her body, her yellow eyes fixed on Virginia's back. Lavinia noticed the cat and kept quiet.

Virginia took the pendant from Ian and refastened it around her neck. She slowly sipped her wine, then turned toward Peggy and saw the cat's eyes glowing in the candlelight. Virginia's hand went to her throat. She began making gagging noises. She left the table, then ran into the house and out the front door.

Without a word, Stu jumped up and followed Virginia.

Peggy picked up the cat. "I'll be right back. I know I closed this cat in the bedroom before dinner. I can't imagine how she got out."

When Peggy came back into the yard, Chuck and Lavinia were saying good night to Ian. "Thanks for dinner,

Peggy, see you tomorrow." They went through the gate and into their own house.

"Nice neighbors," said Ian. "Have you lived next to each other long?"

"All of our lives. Lovey and I grew up in these houses." Peggy began clearing the table.

"Let me help you," said Ian.

Peggy washed; Ian dried. Soon the kitchen was clean, except for the lasagna pan soaking in the sink.

The grandfather clock bonged the half hour.

"I'd better go," said Ian. "I've got work to do at the shop before we open tomorrow."

Peggy walked Ian to the front door. He kissed her softly on the cheek, then strolled into the night.

CHAPTER 30

"MOM, WHAT AM I GOING TO WEAR TO SCHOOL? Should I wear my baseball uniform?"

Costumes for the boys. Missy forgot to order costumes for the boys on the baseball team, Peggy thought. I wonder what else will go wrong today? "Wear what you usually wear to school. Better hurry, Nicky, you're going to be late."

When Nicky had left for school, Peggy dressed in her colonial costume, making a face at the mirror when she put on the ruffled cap. Nicky would say I look like a dork, she muttered to herself.

She picked up her purse and put it down. A canvas shoulder bag doesn't work with this outfit. What did colonial women use? Peggy laughed to herself. Why did colonial women need purses? Not for car keys or cosmetics or wallets or checkbooks or grocery coupons or sunglasses or any of the other stuff I haul around daily. Who needs a purse when you spend most of your time at home or in the fields? Peggy solved the problem by putting her shoulder bag inside a small wicker basket she could carry on her arm.

What to do about the cat? Tom's Tools was only three

blocks from her house, but it was too late to drive and too far to walk in a long skirt, in unfamiliar flat shoes that were already putting blisters on her heels, while carrying a basket on each arm. She put out fresh food and water for Buster and Pie, hoping they'd behave and not kill each other.

Any other time Peggy would have reached Tom's Tools in five minutes from the time she locked the front door of her house. But with the long skirt wrapping around her legs like eelgrass, the basket banging into her hip, and the shoes rubbing on her feet, the trip took closer to ten minutes. *Tomorrow I'll leave the costume in the store and change in the back room.*

She looked at her watch. Fifteen minutes until flag raising. The watch. Watches were on Max's no-no list. She slipped it off her wrist and put it in her apron pocket.

She stepped out of Tom's Tools to cross over to Ian's Booke Nooke just as the first horse-drawn buggy was making its way up Main Street. Peggy waved at the tourists while cameras clicked. She hoped they were getting their money's worth.

Ian's shop was still closed. No sign of him in Clemmie's Café either. Peggy walked to the town square, where the other costumed residents were gathered around the flag pole. The nearby horse trough had been cleaned of the dead leaves and used candy wrappers and was once again flowing with fresh water. A new brass plaque—the one that the President had given to the town at the ribbon-cutting ceremony—was a focal point for picture taking.

Promptly at nine, Stu raised the flag and everyone sang "The Star-Spangled Banner." Colonial Village was officially open.

"Look, Dad, that flag is all wrong. It's got fifty stars on it." The words were spoken by an eight-year-old boy wearing a blue-and-white-striped T-shirt. Peggy instantly recognized a precocious little troublemaker.

Out of the corner of her eye Peggy spotted Max talking into a small handheld recorder. *Major mistake about the* flag, she thought as she headed back to the hardware store. She picked up her skirt to avoid a steaming pile of horse manure in the middle of Main Street. Mistake number two. If given a choice, she'd rather sidestep potholes than poop.

Peggy decided to close the store and go home for lunch. She had to get out of those damned shoes. For her, the morning had been a financial flop. The Cobb's Landing residents who normally came into Tom's Tools were busy being buggy drivers or tour guides, running the ticket booths and concession stands, or tending their own shops. The tourists weren't interested in tools, hardware, or small appliances; they were looking for bathrooms and drinking water. Peggy decided to give them what they wanted. For a price.

She went home, tossed her costume into a shopping bag, and put on her jeans, T-shirt, and oh-so-comfortable backless sandals. Carefully avoiding Main Street, she drove to the nearest supermarket and stocked up on small bottles of water and assorted soft drinks. Getting to the loading dock behind Tom's Tools without violating the Main Street car curfew was like running a maze. But by two, she had a cooler full of ice and soft drinks propped next to the front door, with backup stock chilling in the refrigerator in the back room. She quickly lettered a sign COLD DRINKS, $1.00 EACH and stuck it in the front window. Peggy was back in business.

Nicky and Charlie bounded into the store after school. "Mom, this is so cool with the horses and everything. Did it look like this when you were a little girl? Can we go play down at the river?"

"Be careful and be back here by five."

Lavinia came in at four-thirty dressed in jeans, T-shirt, sunglasses, and a floppy hat that covered most of her face.

"Lovey, what are you supposed to be? Where's your costume?"

"Today this is my costume. I'm pretending I'm a tourist. Get a look at you." She stood back to get the full effect. "Not bad, except for . . ."

"I know. The hat," said Peggy.

"It makes you look like a dork."

"Just wait until tomorrow, smarty-pants. Then it's your turn."

"I come bearing gifts." Lavinia handed Peggy a small wrapped package.

"What's this?"

"Beats me. Ian asked me to give it to you. I feel like John Alden."

"I think you mean Miles Standish."

"Whatever."

"When did you see Ian?"

"A few minutes ago, when I popped into the Booke Nooke. Ian said to tell you he would have delivered it in person, but he's been too busy all day to get across the street." Lavinia fanned her face with her hand. "I can certainly see why. Have you seen him in his costume? He looks like he stepped right out of a history book. That man is hot. No one I know smells that good. The books were flying off the shelves." Lavinia glanced across the street then back at Peggy. "Aren't you going to open the package? I'm dying to see what he gave you."

"Later. Right now I'm going to close up and get out of here. The boys stopped by after school. They wanted to play at the river. I said it was okay."

"I'll meet you down there," said Lavinia. "Don't be too long. Get rid of that hat."

Peggy stuck out her tongue. Lavinia laughed as she left the store and headed across Main Street.

When Lavinia was out of sight, Peggy tore the wrapping off the package. Inside was a slender calf-bound volume topped by a note written in perfect copperplate script. In real ink, not ballpoint.

Peggy, I thought you might find this interesting. Ian

Peggy opened the book to its title page: *Memorable Providences Relating to Witchcrafts and Possessions by Cotton Mather (Boston, 1689).*

What were you expecting? A book of Shakespearean love sonnets? This isn't the most romantic gift I've ever received, Peggy thought. In fact, it's downright creepy. Even though it is very old and probably quite valuable. What was Ian thinking? Peggy carefully rewrapped the book and slipped it into her purse before heading down to the Rock River to meet her son.

She found Nicky close to the concession stand.

"Nicky, where did you get that hot dog? And where did you get the money to pay for it?"

"Relax, Peggy," said Lavinia, wiping a dab of mustard off her chin. "Max treated. He's treating everyone."

"A little problem in the hotel kitchen," said Max. "Nothing that can't be fixed by closing the hotel for a few days next week. Have a hot dog, Mayor. I personally recommend the jalapeño relish. It's selling like hotcakes in the hotel gift shop. My own secret recipe."

"Why, Max," said Peggy. "I didn't know you were a whiz in the kitchen."

"I have many hidden talents." With a wink and a wave, Max headed back to the hotel.

"We might as well eat hot dogs," said Peggy. "I have nothing planned for dinner tonight."

They took their food down to the riverbank and sat on a split log bench watching the tourists swim and float on inner tubes. They were joined by Stu and Virginia.

"How did your shop do today, Virginia?" asked Peggy.

"I'm not opening until tomorrow. I didn't think we'd have such a good turnout today so I didn't get anyone to cover for me. Colonial Village wasn't supposed to open until school was out for the summer."

"Doesn't that water look inviting." Lavinia sighed wistfully. "Makes me want to run home and put on my swimming suit. How about it, PJ? Virginia, you can borrow one of mine. We're almost the same size."

"No, thanks," replied Virginia. "I don't swim."

"Not at all?"

"Drop it, Lavinia." Stu put his arm protectively around his bride-to-be.

"Sorry, Virginia. C'mon, PJ. I'm dying for a swim. I might even try out the dunking stool, it looks like a lot of fun."

"Stu, can we go home? I'm not feeling very well," said Virginia.

"I wonder what got into her?" said Lavinia.

"Forget it, Lovey. Where are the boys? My car's parked behind the store. If we hurry, we can get back in time for a swim before sunset."

CHAPTER 31

A SMALL BUT APPROPRIATELY SOLEMN GROUP GATH-
ered at the Cobb's Landing Congregational Church for
Selma's funeral.

"I thought there would be more people here," Peggy
whispered to Lavinia.

"After that stunt her parents pulled? I'm surprised anyone showed up. I feel like a fool sitting here in this stupid
costume. I'll never make it to the cemetery in these shoes."

A voice behind them hissed, "The service is starting."

An hour later they walked down the hill from the cemetery. Tourists stopped reading the inscriptions on the old
tombstones to snap pictures of the two women walking
arm in arm in colonial costumes.

"That was the saddest funeral I've ever been to," said
Peggy.

"It seemed fairly run-of-the-mill to me," replied
Lavinia. "Two hymns, a eulogy, a walk to the cemetery,
and here we are. My feet are killing me."

"That's what made it so sad. The eulogy was a fill-in-
the-blank with the name of the deceased, the pallbearers

were employees of the funeral parlor. You and I were the only people there who really knew Selma."

"Peggy, I don't think we knew her at all. Selma's life was a closed book to everyone. We only saw what she wanted us to see."

"I hope when I go, there'll be someone there who really cares."

"Don't be morbid, PJ." Lavinia stopped to shake a stone out of her shoe. "I promised Chuck I'd help out at the sign shop today. Dinner tonight. Our house. Chuck's firing up the grill for the first cookout of the season."

Peggy normally closed the hardware store at noon on Saturday in order to spend more of the weekend with Nicky. But Nicky and Charlie were busy practicing at the baseball field and she was making money selling sodas. At three, her cooler and refrigerator empty, Peggy locked up and went home.

For the first time in months, Peggy had the house to herself and nothing that really needed doing. Except for laundry. With an active ten-year-old boy in the house, there was always laundry to be done. Peggy tossed a load in the washer.

It was too nice a day to stay inside. She poured a glass of iced tea and went out in the backyard to relax in the swing Tom had made for her the first year they were married. On an impulse, she'd carried with her the book Ian had given her. I know this is going to be deadly dull, she thought, but I might as well skim it so I can say something the next time I run into him.

The type was small, the font broken, and the spellings archaic. All the s's looked like f's. Boston became Bofton. Possession, poffeffion. As Peggy began reading, two names leapt off the pages: Goodwin and Glover. She went back and started at the beginning.

Memorable Providences was Cotton Mather's account of a 1688 witchcraft case in Boston, that predated—and some said Mather's treatise was a handbook for—the 1692 witchcraft trials in Salem.

The Boston case began when thirteen-year-old Martha Goodwin accused a laundry girl of stealing some linens. The girl's mother, Goody Glover, an Irish washerwoman, cursed Martha and her sister Sarah. The Goodwin girls proceeded to exhibit pains, fits, and erratic behavior to the extent that Goody Glover was accused of being a witch and later hanged. Cotton Mather, then in his twenties, took Martha Goodwin into his home for prayer and counseling. Several months later she was considered cured, although it was thought by some that Martha had merely tired of her charade now that Goody Glover was dead.

Cotton Mather, unable to resist publicizing his success under the guise of scholarship, wrote his book describing the case and Martha's symptoms in detail.

> Sometimes they would be Deaf, sometimes Dumb, and sometimes Blind, and often, all this at once. One while their Tongues would be drawn down their throats; another-while they would be pull'd out upon their Chins, to a prodigious length. They would have their Mouths open unto a such Wideness, that their Jaws went out of joint; and anon they would clap together with a Force like that of a strong Spring-Lock. The same would happen to their Shoulder-Blades, and their Elbows, and Hand-Wrists and several of their joints.

It's obvious Cotton Mather never ran into a child who didn't want to go to school, thought Peggy, thinking of Nicky's more creative attempts to avoid school on a day he hadn't studied for a test. Too bad Benjamin Franklin wasn't around in Mather's time. *Spare the rod and spoil the child.* Martha Goodwin sounds like a spoiled brat. A good spanking would have cured her in no time flat. Not that I believe in hitting children, Peggy said to herself.

Peggy put the laundry in the dryer, then pawed through her shoulder bag looking for the notes she'd taken in the old cemetery. When she couldn't find them, she put on her sneakers and headed up the road, being careful to avoid any tourists who'd wandered off Main Street.

Peggy stood at the gravesites of Josiah Cobb and his wife. Elizabeth Goodwin Cobb, 1743–1789. Was it a coincidence that their daughter was named Martha? Or that the funeral she'd attended that morning was for Selma Goodwin Thomas, supposedly related to Josiah Cobb? What if the story was wrong? What if Selma had been a distant relative not of Josiah Cobb, but his wife Elizabeth?

Peggy walked toward Selma's gravesite. She hung back in the shelter of the yew trees, when she spied someone kneeling at the newly covered grave. Someone who had been too busy to attend the funeral that morning. Peggy watched as the mourner buried something in the loosely packed earth covering the grave. She waited until the mourner had left the cemetery, then went and dug the object out of the dirt. In her hand was a gold wedding band made for a woman's finger.

CHAPTER 32

"HOW DO YOU WANT YOUR BURGER, PEGGY?"

Chuck stood at the grill fanning coals that had reached the dusky red glow of grilling perfection. He flinched when a Frisbee sailed past his right ear. "Hey, guys, take that game next door and take the dogs with you."

Nick and Charlie went through the gate into the Turners' backyard, three dogs nipping at their heels. Peggy watched the yellow disk sail back and forth.

"Burger, Peggy?"

"Love one, thanks."

"How do you want it done?"

Peggy snapped back to reality. "Medium." She headed for the Coopers' kitchen. "I'll see if I can give Lovey a hand."

Lavinia handed Peggy a long, sharp knife. "Would you mind slicing the onions? I always hate doing that. Makes me cry every time."

"I think you're supposed to do it underwater or something. I never can remember." Peggy began slicing. "Lovey, we've got to talk later. There's a lot of weird stuff going on here."

"Like what?"

"Honey, where's the meat? I'm ready to start cooking. We're going to lose the coals."

"Hang on, Chuck." Lavinia pulled a plastic-wrapped plate of hamburger patties out of the refrigerator. "PJ, take this out to Chuck, will you?"

"Mom, we're thirsty," said Charlie.

"I made lemonade. Take the pitcher outside. There are glasses on the table. Nicky, ask your mom what she wants to drink."

The Coopers and the Turners had just sat down at the picnic table when a head popped over the fence separating the Coopers' yard from Acorn Lane. It was the eight-year-old boy from the flag raising, still wearing his blue-and-white-striped T-shirt.

"Dad, look. That's the same lady I saw this afternoon. How come she's not wearing that ugly hat and those old clothes anymore? This place is a big fake."

The boy's father poked his head over the fence. "Anyone know where we can find a bathroom?"

Lavinia put down her hamburger and stormed into the house.

Chuck and Peggy ran after her.

"Peggy Jean, I love this town as much as you do," said Lavinia. "But I will not spend the rest of my life living in a goldfish bowl twenty-four hours a day. Get those tourists out of my yard!"

When Peggy went back outside, the tourists were gone.

Lavinia came back to the picnic. Nothing more was said until everyone had finished eating and Charlie and Nick were toasting marshmallows over the coals to make s'mores.

Peggy helped Lavinia carry the dinner dishes into the kitchen.

"Sorry I blew up like that, PJ."

"Don't worry about it, Lovey. It's forgotten."

Chuck came into the kitchen, put his arms around his

wife, and kissed her on the back of her neck. "Everything okay, honey?"

"I'm fine." She turned to her husband. "Chuck, tell PJ what happened this afternoon with that bratty little kid in the striped T-shirt."

Chuck began to laugh. "That kid and his father came into the sign shop. The kid was eating a double-dip ice cream cone, deliberately dripping all over the signs we were making. Lovey asked him to take the ice cream outside and the kid threw a tantrum right there in the store. But you want to know the worst part?"

At that point Lavinia began to laugh. "As his father was dragging the kid out of the shop, the kid threw his ice cream cone on the floor. His parting words to me were, 'You look like a dork in that hat.' I swear I wanted to strangle that kid. PJ, I'm never wearing that stupid hat again. If Missy were still here, I'd give her a piece of my mind. What was she thinking?"

Peggy laughed until her sides ached.

Lavinia had the final word. "I liked this town a lot better when we had it all to ourselves."

She went to her refrigerator and opened the freezer. "I got us something special for dessert tonight." She handed Peggy a cherry Popsicle, then called out to the boys, "Who wants to play cutthroat Monopoly?"

When the boys were asleep and Chuck was nodding over the late news, Peggy and Lavinia sat at the picnic table watching the last of the coals in the grill turn to ash.

"PJ, what were you saying before dinner? About weird stuff going on here?"

Peggy told Lavinia about the book Ian had given her.

"You'll forgive me for saying this, PJ, but I don't think much of Ian's choice of gifts. I thought he had better taste. He looks more like the poetry type to me. What was the book about?"

"Come over to my house, I'll show it to you."

Sitting in her kitchen, Peggy handed Lovey the book, pointing out the similarity in names.

"You can't be serious. We all know Selma was a little wacky, but witchcraft? That's taking things too far, don't you think? It was only a silly part in a play."

"I went back to the cemetery this afternoon, Lovey. You'll never guess what happened." Peggy pulled the gold ring from her jeans pocket and put it on the table.

"What's this? Where did you find it?"

"Stu buried it in the dirt on top of Selma's grave."

"He did what?"

"I saw him. He was kneeling at the grave, then he buried the ring in the dirt."

"Did he see you?"

"No. I hid behind the yew trees until he'd left. Then I went and dug it up."

Lavinia held the ring up to the light, turning it around and around, carefully inspecting the inside. "It's not engraved." She put it next to her own wedding band. "This ring looks brand new compared to mine. I don't think it's ever been worn."

"Lovey, do you suppose Stu carried a torch for Selma all these years?"

"If he did, he had a funny way of showing it. He didn't even bother to attend her funeral. He spent the day helping Virginia at the quilt shop. He was already there, hanging a quilt in the window, when I went to the sign shop after we left the cemetery." Lavinia handed the ring back to Peggy. "What are you going to do with it?"

"Take it back to her grave, I guess. It makes me feel better knowing that someone cared about Selma at the end of her life."

"Even if that someone is engaged to marry another woman. Peggy, you are such an incurable romantic." Lavinia suddenly slapped a palm to her forehead. "I think Max put a hex on us with all this Colonial Village nonsense. It's certainly sapped my brain. You sit here. I'll be right back. Want another Popsicle?"

Lavinia reappeared in Peggy's kitchen a few minutes

later, with a cherry Popsicle in each hand and an envelope tucked under her arm.

"Don't waste your pity on Selma. She screwed this town the same way her parents did. Eat your Popsicle first, before it melts, then read this." ·

"I'll save it for breakfast." Peggy shoved the Popsicle into her freezer, then reached for the envelope. "What's in here?"

"A copy of Selma's death certificate. It says that Selma died of heart failure. But here's the best part." She pulled several legal-sized pages from the envelope.

"What's that?"

"It's a copy of the trust document for Selma's house. I did some more digging at the courthouse the other day after I left the hospital. That's why I was late getting to the town meeting."

"Cut to the chase, Lovey."

"The town got the house upon Selma's death. We don't have to sneak over there at night anymore. We own the place."

"And?" ·

"The town also got all the fixtures and furnishings in the house on the date of Selma's death." Lavinia flipped through the photocopy. "Read this paragraph."

Peggy skimmed the document. "Selma's parents took care of her after all. They fixed it so she'd have a place to live and an income for life."

"Once she sold everything that wasn't nailed down," Lavinia said dryly. "You might say Selma got the mine and the town got the shaft."

"How's that?"

"Read the last paragraph."

"Oh no," said Peggy, shaking her head. "What are we going to do with another museum?"

CHAPTER 33

PEGGY AND LAVINIA PUT ON THEIR COSTUMES, minus the hats and uncomfortable shoes, for their Sunday afternoon stint as volunteers at the Cobb museum.

Their duties consisted of collecting the five-dollar entrance fee, and—as Lavinia put it—answering dumb questions about a bunch of old junk.

When Josiah Cobb left his house and furnishings to the town, there were strings attached to his bequest. The main one was that the house be maintained as a museum. The original bequest came with an ample fund for upkeep, but with inflation, declining interest rates along with rising labor and material costs, that fund was soon depleted. As a public relations gesture, the button factory contributed to the annual maintenance until the factory was closed. Then Cobb House became the town's white elephant.

The Cobb museum was open on Sunday afternoons from one until four from May until October, closed holidays. Volunteer duties were handled on a rotational schedule with no one working more than one Sunday during a season.

On a normal Sunday, they'd be lucky if a dozen people took the self-guided tour of the two-story home.

"I swear, if that bratty kid shows up today, I will strangle him," said Lavinia as she filled the postcard rack.
"Want to flip to see who does door duty first?"

"You do it, I'll handle the rest of the house. I have a
feeling it's going to be a very slow afternoon." Peggy
picked up a dust cloth and a can of spray polish and made
the rounds of the first and second floors, dusting tables,
straightening chairs, securely fastening velvet ropes across
doorways. The layout of Cobb House was identical to
Selma's; but on a much larger scale, minus the modern
conveniences, and with a lot more furnishings.

By two-thirty, thirty-five paying guests had toured
Cobb House.

"Okay, Lovey, it's my turn to sit. You go play room
monitor."

At four, Peggy locked the front door of Cobb House and
sat counting the day's receipts.

"I'm going to the WC before we leave." A small lava-
tory, not available to the public, had been installed for the
use of the volunteers.

"Don't be too long, Lovey. I want to go home and get
out of these clothes."

Peggy finished counting the money—three hundred
and sixty-eight dollars and fifty cents, including postcard
sales at a quarter each—made up a bank deposit, and entered the figures in the ledger. She took the postcards off
the rack and stored them in a chest. What was taking
Lovey so long?

"Peggy, come here! You'll never guess what I found!"

Peggy followed her friend to the library.

"That damned long skirt Missy designed caught on a
nail in the floor and I fell against the bookcase. It's just like
that Nancy Drew book you loaned me."

"Which one? *The Secret of the Old Clock*?"

"No, the next one. *The Hidden Staircase*."

The end of the bookcase had opened to reveal a secret
compartment about the size of a broom closet, or an adult

of colonial weight and stature. Set into the floor of the compartment was a trapdoor.

"Do you think there's a secret passage under there?"

"Give me a hand, Lovey, we're going to find out."

They finally managed to open the trapdoor. To their great disappointment, there was no secret passage waiting. What they discovered was a hidey-hole about four feet square.

The hole was empty.

"All that effort for nothing," said Lavinia, brushing the grime off her hands. "What do you suppose that was used for?"

"The house was built a century too early to be part of the underground railway."

"Perhaps Josiah Cobb was a smuggler and that's where he hid his booty. Who else do you suppose knew about that secret hiding place?"

"None of the volunteers, that's for sure. You know how everyone in this town loves to talk. If anyone had stumbled on it, we would have known the next day."

They looked out of the library window across Acorn Lane.

"PJ," said Lavinia. "Are you thinking what I'm thinking?"

Peggy nodded slowly. "If there's a secret compartment in one house . . ."

"There should be one in the other."

The two women high-fived each other.

"Come on, Lovey. Let's go."

"How are we going to get inside?"

Peggy pulled a key from her apron pocket and dangled it in front of Lavinia's eyes. "I took this from Stu's desk this morning when I stopped at the town office to pick up the keys to Cobb House. When Stu finds out Selma's house now belongs to the town, I don't think he'll have the nerve to say anything to me about it."

After locking up Cobb House, the women walked across Acorn Lane, bold as brass, and let themselves in the back door of Selma's former home.

CHAPTER 34

THEIR HUNCH WAS RIGHT. BUT THIS TIME THE hidey-hole under the trapdoor was a small floor safe with a combination lock.

"I think we've found Selma's safe-deposit box," said Peggy.

"How are we going to get into it?"

"We'll find the combination."

"We could be here forever, PJ."

"Think about it, Lovey. People are predictable. If the numbers aren't something they'll remember easily, like a birthday or social security number, they write them down. What would you pick for a combination?"

"A birthday, I guess. Mine, Chuck's, or Charlie's. Or my wedding date. Or some other date that was really important to me."

"When was Selma's birthday?"

"Beats me, PJ. We didn't exchange cards."

"Well, let's start looking around. There's got to be a clue here somewhere. It wouldn't be her address or phone number, those are too obvious. Where's Selma's purse?"

"I don't know. Didn't Stu say it was found in the river?"

They began their search on the top floor in what had originally been the master bedroom, where the cheap pine double bed and matching dresser were now the only furnishings.

Lovey went through the dresser while Peggy checked the closet.

"We know one thing, PJ. Selma didn't spend much on clothes."

No clues in the bathroom, either.

The rest of the second-floor rooms were empty, except for draperies on the windows. Their footsteps on the hardwood floor echoed in the barren hallway.

They looked in the kitchen, inside the sparsely stocked pantry. Lavinia opened the refrigerator and checked the freezer.

Back through the deserted dining room, living room, parlor, and finally to the library.

"I'm stumped, PJ." Lavinia flopped on the lounger in front of the portable television. "What time is it?"

Peggy pulled her watch out of her apron pocket. "Five-fifteen."

"Let's go home. Chuck and Charlie will be wondering what happened to me. We can come back here tomorrow."

Peggy dropped the watch back into her pocket, where it clinked against Selma's key. She pulled out the key and studied it. "Lovey, there are six numbers stamped on this key." Peggy ran to the floor safe. "Read the numbers to me slowly, two at a time."

Peggy tried the numbers. Left, right, left. Then right, left, right. The lock refused to budge.

Lavinia looked around the library, her eyes resting on the built-in fireplace. She got out of the lounger and knelt before the fireplace, staring at the hearth.

"Peggy, look. The combination has been in plain sight the entire time." She laughed. "You could say it's been right under our feet." She pointed to the hearthstone, where a stonemason had long ago chiseled: JOHN MARTIN AND MARTHA COBB, WEDDED THIS DAY OCTOBER 16, 1780.

Ten. Sixteen. Eighty. The floor safe at last revealed its contents.

Lavinia looked over Peggy's shoulder. "You weren't really expecting to find gold, jewels, and wads of cash in there, were you?"

Peggy looked down at the bundles of receipts, ledger books, and other assorted papers and envelopes that filled the safe.

"I told you last night, PJ, whatever there was of value in this house, Selma converted to cash a long time ago."

"Lovey, see if you can find some sturdy shopping bags or boxes in the pantry. I'm taking all these papers home with me. If the town got screwed again, I'd like to find out how badly we were taken."

"We'd better get a move on, PJ. Don't forget, Max has fireworks planned for tonight."

CHAPTER 35

"C'MON, MOM. WE'RE GOING TO BE LATE FOR THE fireworks." Nicky was dancing with excitement. "Will they be better than the ones on TV?"

In a small town where there was no money for teachers' raises or repairs for an aging police cruiser, Fourth of July fireworks were a needless extravagance. Every year a few enterprising souls would go across the state line to buy sparklers and bottle rockets. Every year someone would set off at least one cherry bomb in the horse trough.

Peggy turned a blind eye to the contraband; but she refused, despite Nicky's fervent pleading, to sell fireworks at Tom's Tools. She made an exception for snakes and punk. They were messy but harmless, and the kids loved them.

On the Fourth of July, after a day of baseball games and swimming in the Rock River, the Cooper family and the Turner twosome would usually have a picnic, then watch the Boston and New York fireworks on television. In his ten years, Nicky had never seen a live fireworks display.

Peggy took Nicky's hand. "Let's go, kiddo."

"Aren't we going to drive?"

"Nicky, it's not that far. And there probably won't be anyplace to park at the hotel. We're going to walk."

"Aw, Mom."

They walked over to Main Street, then headed down the street toward the Rock River. Nicky spotted Charlie with some of his teammates. "Okay if I meet you there, Mom?"

"Sure. Run along."

The shops on Main Street were closed for the night, but the horse-drawn buggies were still carrying tourists up Main Street, past the ballpark, around the cemetery, and back down Main Street to the hotel parking lot. All for three bucks a head.

I've got to hand it to Max, thought Peggy, if there's a dollar to be made, he'll find a way to do it. Perhaps Colonial Village wasn't such a bad idea, after all. But will it be enough to put Cobb's Landing back in the black? I guess we'll know more after this weekend.

The riverbank was packed with tourists and residents, filling the log benches, sitting on towels and blankets. The swimmers were all out of the water, and the raft in the middle of the river was being used as a launch pad for the fireworks.

The ticket booth was shutting down for the evening; but because of the problems in the hotel kitchen, business was still brisk at the concession stand.

Peggy reminded herself to make another trip to the discount supermarket to replenish her supply of sodas and water for Tom's Tools.

The hotel parking lot was crammed to capacity. Peggy saw Stu abandon the police cruiser at the end of Main Street when he couldn't find anywhere else to park. He went around to the passenger side to help Virginia out of the car, then locked the door and put the key in his pocket.

Peggy gave Stu and Virginia a wide berth. I shouldn't feel guilty about filching that key from his desk, she thought, but I don't want to get into it with him tonight. She spotted Lavinia waving frantically.

"We saved you a place on our blanket."

"Have you seen Nicky?"

"He's with Charlie. They're over there with their friends." Lavinia pointed to an area of the riverbank where a group of boys were horsing around. "C'mon, Peggy. You don't want to miss the show."

They settled themselves on the blanket. A hum of eager anticipation swept through the crowd as they raised their eyes to the star-flecked darkness above them.

The first rocket exploded in the sky to wild applause, general ohh's and ahh's, and shrill two-fingers-in-the-mouth whistles that grated on everyone's ears.

One by one the fireworks rose in the sky, illuminating the jubilant faces of the watchers on the riverbank in flashes of orange, yellow, white, red, and blue that were reflected in the rippling river. Nicky and Charlie joined their parents on the blanket. Peggy sat cross-legged behind her awestruck son. He looked up at her with sparkling eyes. "Mom, this is the coolest thing I've ever seen."

Twenty minutes into the show there was a brilliant flash of light on the raft. "Get ready for the grand finale," Peggy whispered in Nicky's ear. He quivered with excitement.

Another flash followed. The three men setting off the fireworks dove into the river as the raft ignited like an autumn bonfire. Fireworks exploded everywhere.

The horses spooked and ran driverless up Main Street, empty buggies bouncing behind them on the pavement.

The crowd panicked and ran for their cars. Peggy grabbed Nicky's hand.

One last rocket arced through the sky. It landed on the hood of the police cruiser. Seconds later there was an explosion and the car went up in flames.

There go the weekend profits from Colonial Village, Peggy thought, as she and Nicky ran to see if anyone had been injured.

Chuck and his volunteer firemen sprang into action and soon the police car fire was out; all that remained was a sodden mass of twisted, scorched metal.

When the smoke finally cleared, no one was hurt. Even the horses had come through unscathed.

"Mom, those fireworks were totally awesome," said Nicky. "Can we have them again next year?"

CHAPTER 36

PEGGY HAD WAFFLES WAITING WHEN NICKY CAME down for breakfast on Memorial Day the morning after the fireworks. When he saw the plate, his eyes lit up like Christmas morning.

"What are you doing today, Nicky?"

"We've got practice this morning for the game this afternoon. Will you be at the game?"

"I wouldn't miss it."

"Aren't you going to work at the store?"

"Not today, Nicky. It's a holiday. Don't forget we're going to a picnic tonight after the game. It's a party for your teacher, Miss Morgan."

"She's getting married to Mac."

"Who?"

"Mac. That's what Miss Morgan calls him sometimes." Nicky flushed, remembering his mom's rule about showing proper respect for adults. "I mean, Mr. McIntyre. All the kids at school were talking about it."

Charlie came to pick up Nicky for baseball practice.

"Where's your mom, Charlie?"

"She's still sleeping. My dad told me to be real quiet and not make noise. He went to the sign shop."

"Did you have breakfast?" Without waiting for an answer, Peggy toasted more waffles for Charlie and Nicky.

After the boys left on their bikes for the baseball field, Peggy cleaned up the breakfast dishes, then drove to the supermarket to stock up on sodas and water. She unloaded the cases in the back of Tom's Tools and went home before she got caught out of costume on a day Colonial Village was open.

She had two hours to herself before she had to be at the ballpark. She looked over at the Cooper house. The shades were still down in Lavinia's bedroom.

Peggy took the boxes they'd brought from Selma's house into her living room and sat down on the floor to sort through them.

Boxes, she thought, we all end our lives in boxes. Boxes for our bodies, boxes for all the things we accumulate and hoard throughout the years. I feel like a ghoul prying into Selma's life. Like one of those vulture women shrouded in black from head to toe who stripped the bedroom of the dying woman in that movie with Anthony Quinn and Alan Bates. *Zorba the Greek*, that's it. How would I feel if someone came into my house and started rooting through all my drawers and boxes? I'd hate it. "Absolutely hate it," she stated aloud.

"Hate what?" Peggy looked up to see Lavinia lounging in the kitchen doorway, dressed in shorts and a T-shirt, eating a cherry Popsicle.

"Lovey, are you okay?"

"I've never felt better. I took that Popsicle you were saving. Hope you don't mind. I'll give you another one later."

"Charlie said you were still sleeping, I thought maybe you were sick."

"I decided to give myself the morning off. Don't you ever want to do that? Every day it's get up, make breakfast, get Charlie off to school, go to work, come home, make dinner, do laundry. I wanted to see what it felt like to be a kid again, no responsibilities, no one to think about but myself."

"It's almost noon. Did you just get up?"

"I've been awake for hours. But I spent the morning lolling in bed, reading a trashy paperback. It felt great. Like a minivacation. You should try it sometime. Let me know when, and Nicky can spend the night with Charlie." Lavinia dropped the Popsicle stick in the wastebasket. "You want to do something wild and crazy? Let's drive over to the mall and have lunch in the food court. You drive, I'll buy."

"We'd never make it back in time for the ball game. Nicky's counting on me to be there."

"See what I mean? You, Peggy Jean Turner, need a vacation." She looked down at the unopened boxes. "What are you doing?"

"I was going to start going through Selma's stuff."

"Move over, I'll help you. I want to see what she had and what she got for it." Lavinia picked up a pile of sales receipts and began flipping through them. "Holy crap. Listen to this. 'A Chippendale Carved Mahogany Parcel-Gilt Looking Glass, three thousand seven hundred and fifty-three dollars.' Imagine paying that much for a mirror."

"Here's something else, Lovey. 'A Paint-Decorated Lift-Top-Chest-Over-Drawers, twenty-nine thousand eight hundred and sixty dollars.'"

"That's a teacher's take-home pay for an entire year," said Lavinia.

"Get this, Lovey. 'A Molded Copper Leaping Fox Weathervane, seventeen thousand eight hundred and thirty-five dollars.'"

"That's over fifty thousand dollars for just three items. I don't know whether to laugh or cry. You and I clip grocery coupons to save fifty cents on hamburger while someone else spends eighteen thousand dollars on an old weathervane. Makes me want to run right up and see what

I've got stashed in my attic that might be worth something. How much do you suppose she raked in all together?"

Peggy opened one of the ledgers. "Selma kept detailed lists of everything she sold, room by room." Peggy turned the pages, mumbling under her breath while she kept a tally on her fingers. She closed the book, slowly shaking her head in amazement. "Two. Million. Dollars." Peggy sat stupefied. "Two. Million. Dollars."

"PJ, what do you suppose she did with all that money? From what we saw in the house, Selma didn't have a pot to piss in when she died."

Peggy sat staring into space while Lavinia pawed through the boxes. "She kept all her bank statements. They're from a bank in Boston. Here's one from the Citizen's Bank in Cobb's Landing." Lavinia opened the envelope. "Pin money. That's all she had in her local checking account. Enough for gas, groceries, and cat food."

She tossed the envelope back in the box and pulled out another one. "I wonder what's in here. It's not marked and it feels lumpy." She slid her finger under the flap of the small manila envelope and peered at the contents. She extracted a sheet of paper and unfolded it. After she read it, she grabbed Peggy's arm and thrust the paper under her nose. "Look at this."

Peggy's jaw dropped. "Selma and Stu? Married?" She looked at the date on the marriage license. "That was the Christmas after we all graduated from high school. They must have eloped during Christmas vacation."

Lavinia turned the envelope over and shook it. A gold wedding band fell on the carpet. "This looks like a mate to the one you found at the cemetery. Do you still have it?"

Peggy ran upstairs and returned with the ring. The two were a perfect match.

"What are we looking at here, PJ?"

"Lovey, I think we're looking at two million reasons for murder."

"Murder?" Lavinia repeated the word. "Murder? Peggy, I can't believe it. Not in Cobb's Landing."

"Why not? Ten minutes ago I wouldn't have believed Stu and Selma were married. But we've got the proof right here. Think about it, Lovey. They kept that marriage a secret all these years. Selma dies and suddenly Stu is engaged to Virginia. I'd call that a pretty good motive. That, and all the money he's going to inherit." A smile crossed Peggy's lips. "Looks like Stu can afford to buy his own new police cruiser."

"But we don't know if they stayed married. They could have gotten divorced. Or had the marriage annulled."

"You're right, Lovey. I didn't think of that. I wonder if Selma left a will?"

"Wouldn't the town get the money?"

Peggy went to the kitchen, where she'd stashed the copy of the trust document. "I don't think so, Lovey. It says 'all the fixtures and furnishings in the aforedescribed residence on the date of death of the life tenant.' I don't think fixtures and furnishings include money. Anyway, the money wasn't in the house, it was in a bank."

"Stu and Selma. Married. Wait until I tell Chuck."

"Lovey, you can't tell anyone about this. Not even Chuck. Remember what Benjamin Franklin said."

"What's he got to do with it?"

"Franklin said: 'Three can keep a secret, if two of them are dead.'"

"That's really twisted, PJ."

"Promise me you won't breathe a word to anyone. Not until we find out more. If we're wrong about this, we'll look like utter fools; if we're right, we could be tipping off a killer."

"Okay. I promise. But I'm going to have a hard time looking Stu in the face. What are we going to do at that picnic tonight?"

"We're going to act as if none of this ever happened. Come on, Lovey. Help me carry these boxes upstairs. We're going to be late for the ball game."

CHAPTER 37

"IF I HAVE TO SMILE AT STU AND VIRGINIA ONE more time, I swear my face is going to crack," Lavinia muttered to Peggy while they waited for burgers and corn at the grill.

"Half an hour and we can go home."

"What excuse will we give?"

Peggy grinned. "School day tomorrow."

"Brilliant. I wish I'd thought of that an hour ago."

The Turners and the Coopers were getting ready to leave the picnic when Virginia approached. "Is everyone getting enough to eat?"

"Great party, Virginia," said Peggy. "Thanks for inviting us."

"You can't leave yet."

"It's a school night."

Lavinia covered her smile with a cough, then told the boys to go wait in the car.

"Mac, honey, Peggy and the Coopers are leaving," said Virginia. She turned back to Peggy. "We wanted to talk to you about the wedding. Max came up with a wonderful idea. He wants us to have the wedding in the town square on the Fourth of July. He said he'd pay for everything. Even the honeymoon. Anyplace we want to go. Isn't he generous?"

"To a fault," said Peggy. "But how does this concern us?"

"We"—Virginia leaned back against Stu—"want you, and Chuck and Lavinia, to be in the wedding party. It would mean everything to us. Please say you will. It would make the wedding perfect."

"The icing on the cake," said Lavinia.

"Exactly," said Virginia. "As Max said, if you're only going to do it once, do it right."

An hour later, after the boys had gone to bed, Lavinia went over to Peggy's house. "I brought you a Popsicle. Eat it before it melts." After Peggy had torn off the wrapping and was nibbling the cherry ice, Lavinia said, "How could you agree to be in that wedding?"

"You agreed, too, Lovey. You and Chuck. How were we going to get out of it? Say we were busy that day? We'd already made plans to watch paint dry or rotate our tires?"

Lavinia giggled.

"What did you want me to say? Don't count on a wedding, Virginia, because your fiancé might be in jail for the murder of his first wife?" Peggy licked the cherry juice dribbling off the end of the wooden stick. "What's with this Mac business? I don't remember anyone ever calling Stu anything but Stu."

"Only Selma," replied Lavinia. "Mac was her pet name for Stu when we were in high school." She pointed her finger to her throat and began making gagging noises.

Lavinia went home, leaving Peggy in her kitchen, feet up, eating the Popsicle. But in Peggy's head, wheels were turning. She dropped the stick in the wastebasket, locked up for the night, and went up to her bedroom. She took Selma's boxes out of her closet and put them on her bed.

The eastern sky was turning pink when Peggy repacked the boxes and put them back in her closet.

Two million dollars. Kaput. Vanished in brokerage fees

and a dot com bubble gone bust. As far as Peggy could tell, all Selma had left when she died was the meager balance in her Citizen's Bank checking account. Pin money.

Two million dollars. Peggy thought about it as she went downstairs to the kitchen to make coffee, Pie padding softly behind her. With Pie purring on her lap, Peggy sat drinking coffee, doodling on a notepad. It was easier to think about a million dollars. What was a million dollars? One thousand thousand-dollar bills. In that context it didn't seem like much. More like Monopoly money. But at five percent simple interest, a million dollars would generate fifty thousand dollars every year. Two million dollars, one hundred thousand in interest. Before taxes. I could live on that interest. I'd go back to college, get a degree in library science. Put more money in Nicky's college fund. Thinking about what to do with the interest on two million dollars was a pipe dream. Like winning the Powerball lottery. Nicky and I are doing just fine without it. After all, two million dollars hadn't done Selma much good.

Peggy picked up Pie and went into the backyard, where Buster was chasing squirrels. Putting money out of her mind, she thought instead about Selma and Stu. And thought about her conversation with Selma in the post office. What was it Selma had said? "There's something you should know about Max," was the way Peggy remembered it. Which really didn't make much sense. What if Selma had really said, "There's something you should know about Mac." Max, Mac. The two names sounded very much alike.

What did Selma want to tell her about Stu? That they were married? Did Stu want out of his marriage to Selma so he could marry Virginia? I could understand this better if Selma still had money, thought Peggy. Money is always a good motive for crime. But Selma was broke. All Stu gained from Selma's death was his freedom. Perhaps that was a sufficient motive for murder. People did strange things for love. A king had once given up his throne. True crime novels were full of crimes of passion; men killing

their wives to be with another woman, women slipping
poison to their husbands or paying to have them murdered.
A talk with Stu was definitely in order, but did she have
enough evidence to accuse him of anything?

All Peggy knew for sure were two things: Selma had
been married to Stu. Selma was now dead.

Everything else was speculation. Where did Selma die?
In the cemetery? Peggy remembered the eerie cry of the
screech owl the night of the eclipse as she sat in her car
waiting for Selma to show. What if that had been Selma's
death cry? The very thought made Peggy shiver.

How did Selma die? It was convenient to think that the
scratches she'd photographed on the trunk of the yew tree
were made by Selma's fingernails and the dirt under her
nails was really yew bark. But was it the truth? Even
though the medical examiner listed heart failure as the
cause of death on the certificate, Peggy wondered if he had
used that as a pat solution to a problem that was beyond his
ability to solve.

How did the body get from the cemetery to the waterwheel? And why was it taken there? So it would be more
easily discovered? There were far more conspicuous
places to put a body in Cobb's Landing. The town square,
for starters. The horse trough was big enough to hold a
body Selma's size. Why the waterwheel? Because it was
part of the button factory? Put the body there as a final reminder to the town that her parents had skipped with the
pension fund? It was the best reason Peggy could think of
for moving the body to the waterwheel.

Where to go from here? What would Nancy Drew do?
Peggy knew the answer to that question. Nancy would get
off her trim backside, hop into her roadster, and go looking
for clues. But Nancy didn't have a ten-year-old son to feed
and get off to school or a business to run. Peggy went into
the house to make breakfast for Nicky and plan the rest of
her day. High on her list was a talk with the medical examiner.

CHAPTER 38

WHILE SHE WAS OPENING TOM'S TOOLS, PEGGY spotted Ian outside the Booke Nooke. As she crossed Main Street, she pulled the book he'd given her from her bag.

"Ian, I want to thank you for this. It was very thoughtful of you, but I can't keep it. This book belongs in a museum or rare book room."

"I want you to have it. It's not an original printing, it's a facsimile edition."

"Really?" Peggy turned the book over in her hands. "It looks and feels like an original." A curious expression crossed her face.

"Peggy, are you all right?"

"Ian, you've given me a great idea." Peggy threw her arms around him and kissed his cheek. "Thank you. I've got to run, I'll talk to you later."

Her next stop was the county hospital for her appointment with the medical examiner. A very illuminating half hour. As she was leaving the hospital, she heard a familiar voice calling her name.

"PJ, wait up!"

She stopped and waited for Lavinia.

"Is everything all right? Nothing's happened to Charlie or Nicky?"

"Relax, Lovey. The boys are in school. I came here to see the medical examiner."

"What did you find out?"

"Tell you later."

Lavinia stuck out her tongue as Peggy hopped in her car.

The third stop on Peggy's list was the library. She returned the books she'd checked out on yews, then headed for the reference section. After an hour of research and feeding ten dollars' worth of quarters into the copy machine, she felt as if she'd hit the jackpot. Max. She needed to talk to Max.

Last on her morning list was the stop Peggy dreaded. She drove back to Cobb's Landing for a meeting with Stu.

He was sitting at his desk when she walked into the police station. "Peggy, I know what you're going to say. It was all my fault."

Peggy kept her mouth shut and let Stu continue.

"If I hadn't parked the police cruiser illegally, it wouldn't have been hit by the firework and demolished."

"What am I going to do, Stu? Give you a ticket? Take the cost of a new cruiser out of your pay?"

"Geez, Peggy. Don't you think that's going too far?"

Peggy took a deep breath. "No, Stu. I think lying is going too far. I went to see the medical examiner this morning. He told me some very interesting things." Peggy reached in her purse, then dropped the wedding ring on Stu's desk. His face blanched and his hands began to tremble.

"I also think murder is going too far. I'm relieving you of your duties, pending further investigation. As of this minute, you're on paid suspension. Give me your badge."

Stu unfastened the badge from his shirt and put it in Peggy's outstretched hand.

Peggy put the badge in her purse. On her way out the

door she turned to Stu. "If you talk about this, and you probably will, see that you get your facts straight."

It was noon when Peggy finally opened the hardware store; by one, everyone in Cobb's Landing knew that Stu was on suspension but didn't know why; by two, Peggy was the town pariah; by three, there was talk of a recall petition and a special mayoral election; at four, Virginia Morgan stormed into Tom's Tools.

"Peggy Jean Turner, you've gone too far. I told Stu to hire a lawyer and sue you for everything you've got. You haven't heard the last of this. If Stu doesn't get even with you, I will." As her parting shot, Virginia said, "You can forget about being in our wedding party. I don't want to be in the same room with you."

CHAPTER 39

NICKY CAME HOME FROM SCHOOL IN TEARS. "MAC, I mean Mr. McIntyre, kicked me off the baseball team."

"He what?"

"He said no son of a slanderer was going to play on his team."

"He did, did he? We'll see about that."

"Mom, what does slanderer mean?"

"We'll talk about it when I get back."

Peggy broke all speed limits getting to Stu's house. Stu answered the door, dressed in a suit and tie. "My lawyer told me not to talk to you."

"This isn't about your lawyer, Stu. It's about my son. You will not take your personal problems out on Nicky. He will be at baseball practice tomorrow and he will be allowed to play. You can tell Virginia that if she has any plans to give Nicky a hard time in class or on his final report card, she'll have me and the school board to deal with. Tell that to your lawyer."

Peggy slammed her car door and drove home at a crawl, minding the speed limits.

"Nicky, it's all fixed. You go to baseball practice

tomorrow like you always do. If anyone gives you any trouble, you come and tell me."

"Mom, why is Mr. McIntyre mad at you? I thought you were friends."

Peggy chose her next words very carefully, knowing she couldn't tell Nicky anything he might accidentally repeat to the other kids. "Sometimes friends have disagreements. You and Charlie are friends. Do you always agree on everything?"

Nicky thought for a moment. "No. He likes strawberry ice cream. I hate it."

"But you're still friends?"

"Sure."

"Nicky, remember a couple of years ago when Charlie got a new baseball for his birthday? And you brought it over here to play with and left it in the backyard? And Buster chewed it?"

Nicky nodded.

"Were you and Charlie friends then?"

"He was pretty mad at me."

"Then what happened?"

"You made me save my allowance to buy him a new ball."

"After that?"

"We were good friends again. Are you mad at Mr. McIntyre because he's going to marry Miss Morgan?"

"Of course not. Who told you that?"

Nicky shrugged. "Nobody. I just wondered. Can we have supper now? I'm hungry."

"I'll set the table while you go get your dictionary."

Nicky came back with his dictionary. While they ate, Peggy and Nick discussed the word "slander" and the difference between slander and libel. "Can we drop it, Mom? This is more boring than English class."

Peggy knew she'd made a muddle of it. "Nicky, go ask Charlie if he wants to come to the general store with us for ice cream."

Lavinia decided to walk with them. "PJ, we've got to

tell Chuck what's going on. I've kept my promise to you, but Chuck doesn't understand what you did today. He thinks you've slipped your trolley."

"You're right, Lovey. It's time we told him. And I've got something else I want to talk to Chuck about."

Chuck listened quietly while Peggy and Lavinia told him about Cobb House and then finding the hidey-hole in Selma's house. Peggy pulled the marriage license from her purse along with the wedding rings.

Chuck looked at the marriage license and let out a low whistle. "Stu and Selma, married? That sly dog."

"Not only that, honey," said Lavinia. "Selma was worth two million dollars when she died."

"Hell, I would have married her for two million dollars," said Chuck.

Lavinia slapped his hand.

"Forget about the money," said Peggy. "It's all gone."

Lavinia turned to Peggy. "How did you find that out?"

"I was up all night going through the boxes. Selma put the money in the stock market and lost it all when the market went bust."

"That lets Stu off the hook, right? If Selma didn't have any money, Stu had no reason to kill her for it," said Lavinia.

"Wait a minute," said Chuck. "Who said anything about anybody getting killed?"

"We think Selma was murdered, Chuck," said Peggy.

Chuck turned to Lavinia. "I thought you said Selma died of heart failure."

"That's what was on the death certificate," said Lavinia.

"The death certificate was misleading," said Peggy, putting a copy of the certificate on the table. "I talked to the medical examiner this morning. Heart failure is probably what killed Selma. But what caused it? A week ago I told Stu about the yew trees in the cemetery, and he promised to tell the medical examiner. He never did. Look at the

certificate. It says Selma was never married. Where did the
medical examiner get that information?"

"From Stu?" said Lavinia.

Peggy nodded.

Chuck shook his head in disbelief. "You think you
know someone all these years. Stu and I used to play ball
together when we were kids, the way Charlie and Nick do
now."

"Stu's been lying to us all along," said Peggy. "He lied
about not knowing if Selma still had a cat—I found cat
hair matching Pie's on his shirt before we went to Selma's
house to rescue the cat. He lied about Virginia's allergy to
cats. Virginia came into the hardware store when Pie was
under the counter, and the night we had the dinner at my
house Pie was sitting on the picnic table for at least two
minutes. Virginia didn't have a problem until she actually
saw the cat. I think that allergy is a fake. Stu lied to the
medical examiner about Selma's marital status. Do you
want me to continue?"

Chuck shook his head. "It still doesn't mean he killed
her."

"Try this." Peggy pulled a plastic bag out of her tote. Inside the bag was a water-stained leather purse. Peggy
opened the purse and extracted a small date book, a
Christmas giveaway from the Citizen's Bank. Selma's
name was written on the flyleaf. "On the night she died,
Selma was meeting Stu at seven. It says so right here."

"Where did you get that?" asked Lavinia.

"From the medical examiner. He fished Selma's purse
out of the river the morning her body was found."

"It still doesn't prove Stu killed her," said Chuck.

"No, but he may have been the last person to see her
alive," said Peggy.

"Where were they meeting?" asked Lavinia.

"It doesn't say."

"I don't like any of this, Peggy, but I think you did the
right thing by suspending Stu until we find out who killed
Selma," said Chuck. "I'll talk to Stu tomorrow. See what

he has to say for himself. Come on, Lovey, let's go home. It's late."

"PJ, you said you wanted to talk to Chuck about something else?"

"It'll keep."

CHAPTER 40

"WELL, MAYOR, IT LOOKS LIKE YOU'VE GOT YOURSELF in a pretty pickle." Max breezed into Tom's Tools the following day about noon. "I'd say you've slipped a few points in the popularity polls."

"Thanks for telling me." Peggy hadn't made a sale all morning. "What's on your mind, Max?"

Max handed Peggy a check. "It's the town's take from the weekend. It might cover the down payment on a new police cruiser. If you need a loan to cover the balance . . ."

"I know, Max." Peggy smiled as she said the next words. "You'll make me an offer I can't refuse."

"You wound me, Mayor." Max clutched his chest, a gesture Peggy had seen before. "That's not how I operate. You've been watching too many old movies."

"Max, how would I go about getting a business loan?"

Max looked around Tom's Tools. "Are you thinking of expanding? If I were you, I'd get more customers first."

"I've got something else in mind."

"Get your problems with the police officer and that other mess cleared up, then bring me your business plan. Right now you're not a very good credit risk."

"Not a good credit risk? Max, you just offered me a loan for a new police cruiser."

"That offer wasn't for you personally, Mayor, that was for the town." With a barely discernable flick of his fingers, Max was gone.

Looking for a friendly face, Peggy headed across Main Street to the Booke Nooke. On the shop door was a notice in Ian's distinctive script: *Off on a buying trip, open Friday.*

No one sitting in Clemmie's Café looked up as Peggy walked past. I'm being shunned, Peggy thought as she went back to the hardware store. I wonder if this is how Selma felt after her parents left Cobb's Landing with the pension fund.

Peggy closed up early. There was no point sitting at Tom's Tools waiting for customers who weren't going to come.

She stopped at the town office, a room behind the police office, to get a deposit slip for the check she needed to deposit into the town's operating account.

Peggy walked in on Lavinia and Chuck talking to Stu.

"Peggy, we didn't expect to see you here," said Lavinia.

"Max gave me a check from last weekend's take for Colonial Village. I came to pick up a deposit slip." Her voice faltered. "I wasn't aware we had a town meeting scheduled."

Lavinia looked at Stu and Chuck, then turned to Peggy. "I'll take that check, Peggy. And your key to the office."

"What's going on here?"

"The town wants to reinstate Stu as police chief and suspend you as mayor, pending a new election. Here are the petitions." Lavinia pointed to a folder stuffed with signed petitions.

Peggy opened the folder. Just as she'd suspected, the person behind the drive to oust her and reinstate Stu was none other than Virginia Morgan.

Peggy turned to Lavinia. "I guess that makes you the interim mayor."

Lavinia looked miserable.

Peggy took the key to the town office off her key ring and handed it to Lavinia together with the check from Max.

"One more thing? Stu's badge?"

Peggy dug in her purse for the badge and put it on Stu's desk. She left without saying another word.

Now what to do? In her heart Peggy wanted to get even by going to Virginia and spilling the beans about Stu's marriage to Selma. But something held her back. She'd had enough of Virginia Morgan for the time being. Let Stu dig his own grave. Peggy went to the baseball field, arriving just as practice was ending. Stu was nowhere to be seen.

Nicky was happy with the way practice had gone and glad to see her. They got in the car and went out for a fast-food dinner and an early movie, arriving home just before ten.

As Nicky was heading upstairs to bed, there was a knock on the kitchen door. Lavinia stood outside with a bottle of beer in each hand.

"May I come in? Peggy, we've got to talk."

"Lovey, in all the years I've known you, you've never waited for an invitation to come into this house." Peggy opened the door.

Lavinia handed Peggy a cold beer. "I feel terrible about what happened today." The women sat down at Peggy's kitchen table.

"What did happen today? I still haven't figured it out."

"Chuck and I had a long talk with Stu. He told us all about his marriage to Selma. Selma had Stu under her thumb from the time they started dating in high school."

"Really?"

"Stu married her during Christmas vacation, Selma's freshman year in college. They eloped. You can guess why."

"Don't tell me Selma was pregnant."

"Or said she was. Anyway, she conveniently was no

longer pregnant a month later. But Stu was so hooked on Selma that he agreed to keep their marriage a secret. She said her parents would disown her if they ever found out. But she was coming into some money of her own when she turned twenty-one. You know what happened next."

"Selma's parents skipped town with the pension fund before her twenty-first birthday."

"Bingo."

"Why didn't they start living together in her parents' house?"

"Selma fed Stu a story about having seen her parents' will and that she would inherit the house when they died, provided she was still single."

"He bought that?"

"Hook, line, and sinker. Of course, at that point everyone in the town was furious about what her parents had done and Selma was being treated like an outcast. Stu figured it wouldn't do him any good if the marriage was made public."

"She never told him about the trust."

"Obviously not, PJ."

"Why did they stay married?"

"Stu was still in love with her. He said they used to meet every couple of weeks at a motel outside of town."

"I'm surprised she didn't rent the room by the month instead of the hour."

Lavinia grinned.

"After all those years, when did the snake finally slither into Eden?"

"When Selma went broke. She started hitting Stu up for money. Little sums at first, enough to pay a bill while she waited for a check to clear. One feeble excuse after another. Pretty soon she was expecting money from him every time they got together."

"Lovey, there are names for women like that."

"That's when Stu realized Selma had been conning him all along."

"Wake up and smell the French roast. What did he do?"

"He started seeing Virginia. The last time he met Selma, he told her he wanted a divorce. He says Selma agreed, provided he gave her a big lump-sum settlement. After all, she'd given him the best years of her life."

"Lovey, this is the most incredible story I've ever heard. How could any man be that dumb?"

"Let's not go there. Selma was a very sexy woman when she got herself all tarted up. Enough said."

"Don't tell me he agreed to pay her off?"

"He said he'd think about it and get back to her."

"When was that?"

"The night she died."

"My, my, my." Peggy sat peeling the label off her beer bottle while she thought about everything Lavinia had just said. "So Stu didn't want to get Selma's money, he wanted to keep her from getting his."

"Exactly."

"No wonder Stu was in such a hurry to get the medical examiner to write the death certificate listing Selma as single. That let him off the hook completely."

"How do you know about Stu and the medical examiner?"

"The medical examiner told me himself. He said Stu was pressuring him, using the Colonial Village opening as an excuse, to get the certificate written and release the body for the funeral."

"Stu admitted he was in Selma's house looking for the marriage license. That's how he got the cat hair on his shirt. He hoped to find the license before anyone else did."

"If he had, we never would have known about the marriage. Did you tell Stu where we found it?"

"Of course not. That's our secret, PJ. I also made Chuck swear he'd keep quiet about it."

"Has Stu told Virginia about Selma?"

"I think he's afraid of her."

"Stu is afraid of Virginia? Why?"

"Virginia's got a temper and she's pretty riled, Peggy.

The teachers' union voted to oust her as president because you never gave the teachers a raise."

"Lovey, you know as well as I do, the town has no money."

"We're making money with Colonial Village. She thinks that money should go to the teachers."

"That's your problem now, not mine."

"I don't want to be the mayor, PJ, not even on a temporary basis. This whole thing is crazy. Virginia ran around getting all those petitions signed to get Stu his job back. But the real reason was to get you out of office. Stu said Virginia wants to run for mayor. According to Stu, Virginia said, 'If Peggy won't give the teachers a raise, I will.'"

Peggy shook her head. "Virginia is welcome to the job. Let her worry about sand and road salt, and how the town is going to pay for a new police cruiser without raising property taxes. Let her worry about unemployment and a shrinking tax base."

"PJ, Virginia can't see past the nose on her face. All she cares about is keeping her power base in the teachers' union. Give the teachers a raise and you'll have your job back."

"Lovey, I can't make a promise I can't keep. But if the idea I have in mind works out . . ." Peggy threw her hands in the air. "Why am I even thinking about it? I'm not the mayor anymore. Why do I care what happens in Cobb's Landing? Nicky's right. We should sell everything and move to Florida."

Lavinia looked shocked. "Peggy, you can't do that. What would I do without you? What would Cobb's Landing do without you? You're the best mayor this town has ever had. Tell me your idea."

"We take Selma's house and turn it into a very special museum. Wait, it's easier if I show you." Peggy ran to get the envelope of copies she'd made at the library. She and Lavinia spent the next half hour poring over the pages.

"Peggy, that's absolutely inspired. It's a whole new industry for Cobb's Landing. Better than the button factory.

I'm going to get Chuck. He needs to hear about this immediately."

The three friends talked until after midnight.

"When can we meet with Max?" asked Chuck, his eyes shining with excitement. "School's out the end of this week, I've got the whole summer free to get working on this."

"There's one little hitch," said Peggy. "Max doesn't want to talk to me until . . ."

"Until what?" asked Lavinia.

"Until this whole mess with Selma is finally laid to rest," said Peggy. "You can tell Stu that if he doesn't tell Virginia about his marriage to Selma in the next twenty-four hours, she's going to hear about it from me. As Max would say, ticktock, ticktock."

CHAPTER 41

"MOM, I'M SUPPOSED TO WEAR A WHITE SHIRT AND black pants for the school pageant tonight," Nicky said at breakfast the next morning.

"You can wear the shirt and pants I bought you last-Christmas."

Nicky focused on stirring his cereal.

"What's the matter?"

"The pants don't fit anymore."

"I'll get you a new pair. Bring the shirt down and I'll wash it."

Nicky concentrated on pushing little cereal donuts around the bowl with his spoon.

"Nicky. What's wrong with the shirt?"

"I got ink on it."

Peggy sighed. "Oh, Nicky, on your good shirt?"

"I'm sorry, Mom, it was an accident. I tried to wash it out."

"It's okay, honey. Does it still fit?"

"The sleeves are a little short."

"Never mind. I'll get you a new shirt, too. Anything

else? Nicky, tell me now. You know how I hate last-minute surprises."

"I need two dollars. It's for a gift for Miss Morgan. The whole class is chipping in."

"What are you getting her?"

"I don't know. A sweater or something. A girl's mom picked it out."

Peggy took two dollars from her wallet and handed it to Nicky. "Don't lose it."

Nicky stuffed the money in his jeans pocket. "I won't lose it, Mom. You're not mad at me about the shirt, are you?" Peggy shook her head, then hugged her son. Nicky hugged her back, then picked up his books and went outside to ride his bike to school.

Peggy cleaned up the kitchen, poured a second cup of coffee, and took it upstairs to drink while she got dressed. *All I need is another time-consuming trip to the mall for Nicky's new shirt and pants. Kids. Why do they always wait until the last minute? At least I don't have to bake thirty cupcakes today.*

She was almost at the cemetery, heading for the road out of Cobb's Landing, when her car began listing and pulling to the right. *Now what?* She stopped, got out to look. A right front flat tire. *Holy crap. Nancy Drew would have changed the tire on the spot, briskly brushed the dirt from her hands, then proceeded on her merry way.* Peggy was in no mood to emulate her childhood heroine. She got back in the car, turned around, and slowly drove—the flattened tire making a distinctive whomp-whomp-whomp sound—two blocks to the gas station.

"You drove on that, Peggy? Hope you didn't ruin the rim."

"It was only two blocks. Can you fix it?"

Bob, the gas station owner, knelt to examine the damage. "Nope. This one's past fixing. You're going to need a new tire. Got a good spare?" He checked the spare tire in the trunk. "This'll do. I'll have it changed for you in a jiff." He walked around Peggy's car. "You really need a new set

of tires, Peggy. These are too slick to be safe. I could have
'em on in fifteen minutes."

With no customers at the hardware store, four new tires
were not in Peggy's budget. "Not today, Bob. Let's go with
the spare."

"Whatever you say, Mayor."

"Haven't you heard? I'm not the mayor anymore."

Bob looked at Peggy in complete surprise.

"You didn't sign the petition to have me recalled?"

"What petition?" Bob called out to a customer pumping
gas at the self-serve island. "Slim, you know anything
about a petition against Peggy?"

Slim shook his head while keeping his eyes on the gas
meter. He stopped pumping when it reached five dollars.

"Someone's been twisting your tail, Peggy," said Bob
as he tightened the last lug nut. "I have coffee with the
boys at Clemmie's every morning. No one's said a word
about any petition. We all think you're doing a great job."
He stood up, wiped his hands on a rag, lowered the jack.
"Let me know when you want those new tires, they're on
summer special. I'll put a set aside for you."

Peggy paid Bob and got in her car.

"See you at the school pageant tonight, Peggy."

Peggy had a talk with herself on the way to the discount
mall. Why didn't I check the signatures on those petitions
myself? Was I wrong to suspend Stu without hard evidence? That's the trouble with living in a small town where
you've known everyone all your life. You think everyone's
life is an open book, that no one has any secrets because
we all know each other too well. What a crock. People in
small towns have secrets; they just hide them better.

Who's got a secret? Selma. Stu. Who else?

Secrets beget lies. Liar, liar, pants on fire. Peggy smiled.
That description fit both Selma and Stu. Too bad I can't
chisel it on Selma's tombstone.

Peggy finished her shopping—black pants and white
shirt for Nicky and, as long as she was in the store, the new
pair of sneakers she'd promised him—and headed back to

Cobb's Landing. An express mail delivery slip was stuck on the front door of Tom's Tools.

She grabbed the slip and walked to the post office. The return address on the express mail label was a bookstore in Boston. This must be a mistake, Peggy thought, I didn't order anything.

She moved to the stamp line and opened the cardboard envelope while she waited. Inside were several sheets of paper. On the top was a color print of a portrait, originally done in oil, of a young girl, about age twelve, sitting in a straight-backed chair, holding a black cat in her lap. Peggy stared at the print. Except for the seventeenth-century clothing, it could have been Selma who'd posed for that portrait. Peggy looked at the back of the print. It was labeled: PORTRAIT OF MARTHA GOODWIN, 1688, ARTIST UNKNOWN.

Peggy was so intent on her reading that she didn't see Virginia Morgan standing in line behind her.

Stuck under the clip securing the remaining pages was a handwritten note: *Peggy, "What's past is prologue." Ian.*

Peggy turned the page to a single-sheet biography of a woman born in Ireland, sent as a slave to Barbados in 1650 by Oliver Cromwell. After the woman's husband died in Barbados, the widow and her daughter moved to Boston, where she worked as a laundress until her death on November 16, 1688. Attached to the biography was a photograph of a plaque in a Boston church remembering Ann Glover as the first Catholic martyr in Massachusetts.

Peggy flipped to the next page. What followed were several pages of genealogy. The begats.

Virginia slipped out of the stamp line and left the post office.

Peggy shoved the papers back in the envelope. I haven't got time for this now, she told herself. It's after one o'clock. I need to get back to the hardware store. She bought a roll of stamps and left the post office, smiling as she envisioned the expression on Nicky's face when he saw his new sneakers.

Virginia sat in her car, watching Peggy. She glanced at her watch. Six hours until show time and she had a lot to do. She started her car and drove back to school.

CHAPTER 42

ON HER WAY TO TOM'S TOOLS, PEGGY STOPPED AT the police station/town office to get another look at the re-call petitions. The doors were locked and Peggy no longer had her key.

Between sales, she spent the afternoon taking inventory and working on her plan for Max. At four-thirty, she closed the store and went home to get Nicky ready for the school pageant. They pulled into the driveway at the same time; Peggy in her car, Nicky on his bike.

"Did you get my shirt and pants?"

"Where's my hug?"

Nicky hugged his mother. Peggy put her arm around Nicky and they walked into the house.

"Mom, I've got to hurry. Miss Morgan said we had to be at the school auditorium at six to practice our song with the music teacher one more time before the pageant starts."

"Nicky, it's almost five. I've got to iron your shirt and pants, make something to eat. We'll never be ready in time."

"That's okay, Charlie said I can ride with him and Mr. Cooper. His mom's coming to the pageant right from work." Nicky opened the sneaker box. "Wow! Thanks, Mom. These are great! Racing stripes and everything. Do the stripes glow in the dark?"

Peggy smiled and nodded.

Nicky threw his arms around her. "I love you, Mom."

"I love you too, Nicky. You run upstairs and take a shower while I iron your new shirt and pants. I'll make you a ham-and-cheese sandwich for supper, but we'll stop at Alsop's for a pizza after the pageant, okay?"

"Okay!" Nicky headed for the stairs.

"Don't forget to wash your hair. And scrub behind your ears!"

While the iron heated, Peggy made sandwiches for Nicky and put them on the table. She ironed his shirt and pants and took them upstairs to his room.

Nicky came down dressed for the pageant in his new shirt, new pants, and new sneakers.

"You look very nice, honey. Eat your sandwich, then go brush your teeth."

Charlie called from outside, "Hey, Nick, you ready? My dad's waiting out front."

Nicky wolfed down his sandwich, ran upstairs to brush his teeth, then bolted down the steps and headed for the front door. "See you after the pageant, Mom."

She went to the front door to wave good-bye and heard Charlie say to Nicky as they got into the car, "Your mom got you new sneakers? Those are really cool. Dad, can I get some like that?"

Peggy went upstairs to shower and dress. The phone was ringing when she got out of the shower. She ran to answer it, leaving wet footprints in the upstairs hall. The only response to her breathless hello was a click on the other end of the line.

Thank heavens we don't have to wear those colonial costumes tonight, Peggy thought as she dressed in comfortable navy slacks and a long-sleeved faux-silk print shirt. She slipped on navy shoes, dusted her cheeks with blush, put on lipstick and her good gold hoop earrings, an anniversary present from Tom the year before he died, then went downstairs for her purse and keys. She had fifteen minutes to get to the school auditorium, park the car, and find a seat before the pageant started.

Everyone on Peggy's block had already left for the pageant. The only sounds on Maple Street were the birds twittering in the trees.

Peggy was opening her car door when she heard a voice softly call her name. She looked up to see Virginia Morgan standing next to her.

In Virginia's hand was a gun pointed at Peggy.

"Get in the car, Peggy. We're going for a ride."

CHAPTER 43

VIRGINIA GOT IN THE BACKSEAT BEHIND PEGGY, her gun pointed against Peggy's neck. "Drive down to the river. You pull anything and I'll pull this trigger. That's a promise."

"Virginia, what's going on?"

Virginia pressed the gun barrel into Peggy's neck. "Shut up and drive."

Peggy backed out of her driveway onto Maple Street, the steering wheel sliding through her clammy hands. She took one hand off the wheel to dry her palm on the car seat.

"Keep both hands on the wheel where I can see them," snapped Virginia.

At the end of the block Peggy turned left onto Acorn Lane, then left onto Main Street. She tried to think of some way she could get help—blaring the car horn incessantly?—but she had all of Main Street to herself; everyone in Cobb's Landing was at the school auditorium waiting for the pageant to start. Clemmie's Café, Ian's Booke Nooke, the Colonial Sign Shoppe, Citizen's Bank all were closed, with only night lights dimly illuminating their interiors. Lighting too low to give any hint of human presence within.

Peggy drove to the end of Main Street. Ahead of her was the darkened hotel on the left, still closed for kitchen renovations, the Colonial Village ticket booth and concession stands on the right, shuttered until the weekend. In the background, the Rock River gurgled and glistened in the rays of the setting sun.

"Park here and get out. Leave your keys, you won't need them." Virginia prodded Peggy with the gun, pressing it into the small of Peggy's back.

They walked single file toward the river. Next to the concession stand were the stocks Max had erected to amuse the tourists.

Locked in the first set of stocks was Stu, his arms and feet held fast by the thick planks of wood. His eyes went wild when he saw Virginia with Peggy, but the tape across his mouth prevented him from speaking.

"That's how we punish men who cheat," said Virginia. She pushed Peggy to the second set of stocks. "This is how we punish nosy women who don't mind their own business."

When Peggy was locked in the stocks, Virginia stood facing her captives. Her eyes flicked from one to the other

Knowing that Nicky was safe at the school auditorium and, if anything happened, Lavinia would take care of him, Peggy decided to go for broke.

"Stu cheated?"

"With that trumped-up tart Selma Thomas." Virginia put the gun on the ground and picked up a small pebble. With deadly aim she pitched the pebble at Stu. It caught his temple in a glancing blow, landing with a soft plop on the ground behind him. Stu winced. A trickle of blood dribbled down the side of his face.

Peggy knew in that instant that Stu hadn't told Virginia the truth about his past. "Stu didn't cheat on you, Virginia, he cheated on Selma."

"Liar!" Virginia reached for more pebbles. "He's engaged to me." She threw another pebble at Stu. He tried to duck, but this one hit his forehead.

"But he was married to Selma."

"Liar!"

A flying pebble grazed Peggy's cheek.

"Stu and Selma were married the Christmas following our high school graduation. They were still married the night Selma died. Ask him, Virginia."

Virginia tore the tape off Stu's mouth. "Speak, infidel."

Stu licked his raw bleeding lips. He swallowed, but his throat was too parched to speak.

"Get him some water, Virginia."

Virginia's eyes glittered. "Later. There'll be plenty of water for both of you." Virginia slapped the tape over Stu's mouth and stood with her face inches from his. "I followed you that night. Followed you to that cheap motel. I sat in the parking lot and waited. Waited until after you'd left. I wanted to see who you were with. Then that tart came out of the motel room, wearing the same locket you gave to me. Selma. The lying tart who killed my mother."

Stu stared at Virginia.

A little voice inside Peggy's head said softly, "What's past is prologue." The penny dropped. Peggy said aloud, "Goody Glover?"

Virginia turned to Peggy. "You're so clever, Peggy Turner. So very clever. Selma wasn't that smart. I had to spell everything out for her."

Stu looked at Peggy, his eyes full of questions.

Virginia continued, her attention focused on Peggy. "I was in the post office the morning Selma arranged to meet you at the cemetery. I heard everything she said to you, Peggy. When we left the motel, I forced Selma to drive to the cemetery and tied her arms around a yew tree. Then we had a nice long talk."

Virginia lapsed into an Irish brogue that became more pronounced with every word she spoke. "She had to pay, pay for the lies she told. Stealing linens. Ann Glover was a poor, uneducated, Irish Catholic in Protestant Boston, but she never stole anything. High-and-mighty Martha Good-win soiled those precious linens, then burned them in the fire and said they'd been stolen. When Ann Glover cursed Martha for her lies and threatened to go to her father with the truth, Martha accused Ann of being a witch. It was Martha Goodwin who was the witch. Martha Goodwin with her playacting of faints and fits. Martha Goodwin should have been hanged for her lies. Spit on and stoned like Ann Glover as she was taken to the gallows, her broken body left hanging from the rope as a lesson to all evildoers."

The dusk-to-dawn lights came on, illuminating the madness in Virginia's eyes and the hatred etched on her face.

When Virginia spoke again, the brogue was gone from her speech. "But I finally got even. With every lie Selma told, I twisted the locket chain a little tighter. She clawed at the tree trunk, gasping for breath. On the last twist the chain broke, but it didn't matter. The real witch was finally dead. After I saw Peggy's car leave the cemetery, I brought Selma's body down to the waterwheel and left it there as a lesson to all the evildoers in Cobb's Landing. You lie, you die."

Virginia dropped the pebbles clenched in her fist and picked up the gun from the ground. "Now it's time for another liar to die."

CHAPTER 44

"PEGGY, YOU REALLY SHOULD HAVE GIVEN THE teachers the raise you promised. Now you'll find out what happens to liars." Virginia pointed the gun at Stu. "Make sure her hands are tied tight to that chair."

Stu checked the knots on the ropes that tied Peggy to the dunking stool suspended over the Rock River.

"Virginia, I didn't lie," said Peggy. "I wanted to give the teachers a raise, but the town had no money."

"Liar! There was money for Colonial Village. Dunk her, Stu. Perhaps the cold water will refresh her memory."

Stu slowly let out the rope fastened to the shore end of the teeter-totter lever holding the dunking stool. As he did, the end holding the chair dipped into the cold dark river.

The shock of the still-frigid water took Peggy's breath away. I am not going to die here, she promised herself. Peggy struggled to free her hands. Then the chair was pulled to the surface. Peggy gasped for breath in the chill night air, her wet clothing clinging to her body like a shroud.

"Do you confess your lies?" said Virginia.

Peggy shook her head, knowing full well that Virginia was past reason, past caring, past anything but revenge.

Virginia screamed at Stu. "Dunk her again."

Peggy quickly inhaled as the chair went underwater a second time. The rushing water felt like icy claws tearing at her body. The very blackness of it was as suffocating as being buried alive. Peggy held her breath as long as she could while working to free herself. I can't last much longer, she thought.

When Peggy was at the point of losing consciousness, she felt hands loosening the ropes around her wrists. She sensed the splash of a heavy object landing in the water not far away.

A strong arm reached across Peggy's chest and pulled her to the surface of the river.

When at last she was breathing normally, Peggy opened her eyes and looked up into Ian's face.

Ian swam to shore towing Peggy alongside him and pulled her up onto the riverbank. "Are you all right?" he asked. Peggy began to shiver uncontrollably. Ian wrapped his arms around her. "Can you make it back to the parking lot?" Peggy nodded, then looked down at her bare feet. Ian scooped Peggy into his arms and carried her to the concession stand. He found her shoes next to the dunking stool and slipped them on her feet.

"Ian, how did you get here?" said Peggy. "You saved my life."

"We can talk about all that later. Right now we need to get to the hospital."

"I'm okay. I don't need to go to the hospital," Peggy said. "I need to get home and out of these wet clothes. Nicky is expecting me at the school pageant. I need to see my son."

Ian pointed to where Stu lay on the riverbank. "He needs medical attention. He's been shot."

"Oh my God," said Peggy. "Is he dead?"

"He's been shot in the leg. He's lost a lot of blood, but I think he'll survive."

"Where's Virginia?" asked Peggy.

Ian pointed to the river, where Virginia's body floated facedown in the water.

Virginia Morgan had been right about one thing. She really couldn't swim.

CHAPTER 45

IT WAS NINE FORTY-FIVE WHEN PEGGY FINALLY reached the school auditorium. The pageant was over and everyone was heading for the parking lot.

"Hey, Mom!" Nicky ran up to Peggy. "Did you like our song?"

Peggy grabbed Nicky and hugged him tight.

Nicky wriggled free, his face pink with embarrassment. "Are we gonna get pizza now? You promised."

They were joined by Lavinia, Chuck, and Charlie.

"Everyone come for pizza at our house," said Peggy. "Chuck, would you mind taking the boys home? Lovey, ride with me to get the pizzas. Nicky, get out of those new clothes the second you get home, okay?"

Peggy and Lavinia got into Peggy's car.

"PJ, why is your hair wet?"

"Lovey, it's a long story."

"You weren't at the pageant, were you?"

"Let's get the pizzas. We'll send the boys over to your house, then we'll talk."

Lavinia dashed into Alsop's and came back with two

extra-large, super-supreme-with-everything-but-anchovies
pizzas.

When they pulled into Peggy's driveway, Ian was waiting outside Peggy's front door.

Charlie and Nicky grabbed one pizza and went over to
the Coopers' house to watch television. Chuck came back
with two six-packs of cold beer.

The adults sat at Peggy's kitchen table eating pizza and
drinking beer.

Lavinia took one bite of her pizza, then put the slice
back on her plate. "I can't stand this. I want to know what
happened tonight."

Peggy looked at Ian.

"You start, Peggy."

Peggy took a deep breath. "Stu's in the hospital with a
gunshot wound in his leg. Virginia's dead."

Lavinia and Chuck were too amazed to speak.

"Virginia killed Selma," Peggy said.

"Over Stu?"

"No, Lovey. Because of something that happened
over three hundred years ago." Peggy drank her beer
while she tried to make sense of everything swirling in
her mind.

Ian put his hand on Peggy's. "I'll tell this part of the
story." He turned to Lavinia and Chuck. "When you mention witchcraft, most people think of Salem and the witchcraft trials of 1692 that began when Reverend Samuel
Parris's nine-year-old daughter Betty and her cousin, Abi-
gail Williams, accused Parris's slave, Tituba, of being a
witch. But the witch hunt really started in 1688 in Boston
when thirteen-year-old Martha Goodwin accused the laundress, Goody Glover—whose first name was Ann—of
stealing some linens. When Goody Glover retaliated by
cursing Martha Goodwin, Martha took her revenge by ac-
cusing Goody of witchcraft. After a trial, Goody Glover
was found guilty and hanged in 1688. Cotton Mather wrote
about it in his book *Memorable Providences* published in

1689. A copy of this book was in Samuel Parris's library in
Salem."

"You gave Peggy a copy of that book," said Lavinia.

Ian nodded.

"We both thought you were more the poetry type," said
Lavinia.

Ian laughed. "I am. But when I was talking to Virginia
the night we all had dinner here in the backyard, I admired
her locket. When she told me Glover was a family name
and her ancestors had emigrated to Salem from Ireland, I
knew Virginia was either confused or lying."

"How did you know?" asked Peggy.

"History and genealogy are hobbies of mine. There
were never any Glovers in Salem. I've studied the Salem
witch trials extensively. One of my ancestors was Samuel
Parris. After the 1692 trials in Salem, he moved his family
to Stowe, Massachusetts. When his daughter Betty married, she lived in Concord. My parents still live in Concord." Ian smiled at Peggy. "I used to play at Walden Pond
when I was a child."

"How did Selma come into it?" asked Lavinia.

"Selma was a relative, on her mother's side, of the
Goodwins of Boston," said Ian. "I didn't really know
Selma Thomas, but when I found the portrait of Martha
Goodwin done in 1688, it seemed there was a faint resem-
blance."

Peggy went to get the express mail envelope Ian had
sent her. She passed the copy of Martha Goodwin's portrait
to Lavinia.

"She's a dead ringer for Selma at that age. PJ, where are
our high school annuals?"

Peggy found the annuals and showed them to Ian.

"Selma Thomas played a witch in your senior class
play? How ironic," said Ian. "It's also ironic that her first
name is an anagram of Salem."

"PJ and I always thought her part was typecasting," said
Lavinia, "but we spelled it with a *b* instead of a *w*."

Ian smiled. "When I discovered that Selma Thomas and

Virginia Morgan were both related to the 1688 witchcraft incident in Boston, it seemed unlikely that they would end up in the same small town by accident."

"Selma's family moved here when she was ten or eleven," said Peggy. "Her father ran the button factory."

"Into the ground," said Lavinia.

"Lovey, that's beside the point," said Peggy. "Eat your pizza, it's getting cold."

"When did Virginia Morgan come to Cobb's Landing?" asked Ian.

"Four years ago," said Chuck. "I was on the school board then. She didn't have much teaching experience, but we were desperate for a fifth grade teacher."

"Did she come here because of Selma?" asked Lavinia.

"I don't think so," said Peggy. "I don't think Virginia made the connection until recently. Selma never knew about it until the night she died. Virginia said so tonight."

"Enough about what happened three hundred years ago," said Lavinia. "I want to know what happened tonight."

"It really began this afternoon," said Peggy. "I was in the post office picking up the express mail envelope Ian sent me with the portrait of Martha Goodwin and Ann Glover's biography. I opened the envelope while I was waiting in the stamp line. Virginia was behind me, reading over my shoulder. She thought I didn't know she was there, but I recognized the scent of her perfume. Also in the envelope were the family trees connecting Selma Thomas with Martha Goodwin and Virginia Morgan with Goody Glover."

Peggy looked at Ian. "I didn't make the connection with the quote on your note until later."

"What quote?" asked Lavinia.

"Ian wrote, 'What's past is prologue.' It's Shakespeare, from *The Tempest*."

"I knew you were the poetry type," Lavinia said to Ian, before turning back to Peggy. "Then what happened, PJ?"

"When I went to get into my car to go to the school pageant, Virginia appeared with a gun in her hand."

"Holy crap," said Lavinia. "Wasn't there anyone around you could call for help?"

"Everyone on our block had already left for the pageant," Peggy replied.

"What happened next?" asked Lavinia.

"Virginia forced me to drive down to the river. When we arrived, Stu was already there. She'd locked him in the stocks. She said that was a punishment for men who cheat."

"Stu finally told Virginia about Selma?" said Lavinia.

"No, I told her after she locked me in the stocks."

Lavinia's mouth flew open. "She did what?"

Ian interrupted. "I'm missing something here."

"Chuck, I think we all need another beer," said Lavinia.

Chuck opened a second round and passed the bottles around the table.

Lavinia turned to Ian. "Stu was married to Selma. They kept the marriage a secret. It's a long story. Peggy can fill you in later." She turned back to Peggy. "Why did Virginia put you in the stocks? Was she insane?"

"Apparently so," said Peggy. "She said that was the punishment for nosy women. Which confirmed that she'd been looking over my shoulder at the post office. That's when I said to her, 'Stu cheated?' I figured I had nothing to lose at that point."

Lavinia put down her beer bottle. "What did Virginia say?"

"She said Stu cheated on her with Selma. She'd followed Stu to the motel the last time he saw Selma."

"Then what?"

"I said to Virginia, 'Stu didn't cheat on you, he cheated on Selma.' That's when Virginia found out Stu was married to Selma."

"What did Stu say?"

"He couldn't say anything, Virginia had his mouth taped shut."

Lavinia sighed, shaking her head slowly. "If only Stu hadn't been such a damned coward, none of this would ever have happened."

"In the end he was pretty brave," said Ian. "But we'll get to that part later."

"What did Virginia do when she found out about Stu's marriage?" asked Lavinia.

"Lovey, she completely flipped out. She ranted on about how Selma had killed her mother. That's when I finally made the connection to Goody Glover in 1688. Virginia talked as though she were Goody Glover's daughter and Selma was Martha Goodwin. Virginia was talking in an Irish brogue. It was eerie."

"What did Stu do?"

"He was too dumbstruck to do anything. Remember, we were both locked in the stocks at the time."

"A captive audience." Lavinia clapped her hand over her mouth. "Sorry, PJ, that just slipped out. Go on."

"Then Virginia told us how she forced Selma to drive her to the cemetery. Virginia killed Selma at the yew tree by choking her with the chain on the locket Stu had given Selma when they were dating in high school. The same locket Virginia was wearing. When Selma was dead, Virginia took the body to the waterwheel and put it there as a lesson to the evildoers in Cobb's Landing. 'You lie, you die,' is what Virginia said."

"I'm horrified to think that Virginia's been teaching our kids all year," said Lavinia. "Was it then that she let you go?"

Peggy shook her head. "Virginia's next words were 'Now it's time for another liar to die.'"

"Virginia shot Stu?"

"No, Lovey. She had Stu tie me to the dunking stool."

Lavinia's hand flew up to her mouth. "Oh my God. Oh, Peggy. Why did Virginia do that?"

"Because I hadn't kept my promise to give the teachers a raise."

Lavinia got up to hug Peggy. "I never dreamed Virginia would take it that far. I'm so sorry. Can you talk about it?"

"It was everything you've ever read or seen about a near drowning. I swear, my life started to flash before my eyes the second time Stu dropped me in the river. While I was trying to free my hands, I kept thinking about Nicky." Peggy began to shiver, and tears streamed down her face. Lavinia held her tight.

When Peggy had run out of tears, she looked around the table. "Promise me you'll never breathe a word to Nicky of what really happened tonight. He's too young to understand. I don't want him to grow up afraid of losing his only parent."

Everyone at the table nodded in silent agreement.

Ian reached over to hold Peggy's hand. "This is where I come in."

Lavinia handed Peggy a wad of tissue. "Blow your nose, PJ." Lavinia dropped the used tissue in the wastebasket. "Your turn, Ian. What were you doing at the river?"

"I drove back to Cobb's Landing from Boston late this afternoon and decided to go for a walk after those long hours on the road. I like walking along the river, especially at night. When I got to the end of Main Street, I saw Peggy's car. Then I heard voices on the riverbank."

"Where were they?" asked Lavinia.

"At the dunking stool," said Ian. "I crept closer as Virginia was saying to Peggy, 'Do you confess your lies?' I saw Peggy tied to the dunking stool. When Virginia screamed, 'Dunk her again,' Stu let go of the rope holding the chair above water."

No one said a word. Ian paused for a sip of beer, then continued. "As Peggy dropped into the river, Stu lunged at Virginia. The gun went off. Stu fell to the ground and Virginia went flying backward into the river. That's when I jumped in the river to free Peggy and bring her back to shore."

"What happened to Virginia?"

"She drowned, Lovey."
"I guess the Puritans were right after all."
Everyone turned to look at Chuck.
"Everyone knows a real witch can't swim."

CHAPTER 46

CHUCK PICKED UP THE EMPTY BOTTLES, THEN opened the last round of cold beer.

"What are we going to tell Charlie and Nicky?"

"About what, Lovey?" asked Peggy.

"What happened to their teacher. We have to tell them something."

"It was an accident," Peggy said firmly. "That's what Ian and I told the medical examiner."

"He was there?" said Chuck.

"Ian called the county police when he called the hospital for the ambulance for Stu," said Peggy.

"A lovers' tiff." Lavinia nodded for emphasis. "We'll say it was a lovers' quarrel with an unfortunate ending. That sounds logical to me."

"I can buy it," said Chuck. "I'm going to check on the boys. I'll be right back."

Lavinia sat sipping her beer.

Peggy picked at the topping on a cold piece of pizza. Ian moved closer to Peggy and put his arm around her.

Chuck returned with the second pizza box in his hands. "There's more pizza here if anyone's hungry. The kids are fine. They fell asleep in front of the television. I left them there. It won't matter much if they don't sleep in their own beds tonight. Tomorrow's the last day of school."

"Will someone fill me in on Stu and Selma?" asked Ian.

"They were an item in high school," said Chuck.

"He took her to the senior prom," said Lavinia. She paged through the high school annual. "Here they are."

Ian studied the photo. He turned to Lavinia. "That's you and Chuck, isn't it?" He looked again. "Peggy, who are you with?"

"That's Tom."

"Your late husband?"

Peggy nodded.

"Are you married, Ian?" asked Lavinia.

Ian shook his head.

"Engaged?"

"No."

"Lovey! Stop prying." Peggy kicked Lavinia under the table.

Lavinia grinned like the Cheshire cat.

Peggy cleared her throat. "Stu said they broke off the relationship a few months after high school graduation when Selma came home from college for Christmas vacation."

"But he lied," said Lavinia. "That's when they eloped."

"Why keep the marriage a secret?"

"According to Stu," said Lavinia, "that was Selma's doing. When it turned out she wasn't pregnant, and who knows if she ever really was, she told Stu her parents would disown her if they discovered she was married." She turned to Chuck. "Didn't Stu mention a trust fund or something like that?"

"The golden rule," said Ian.

They waited for Ian to elaborate.

"He who has the gold makes the rules."

Everyone smiled.

"But," said Peggy, "here's where it gets interesting. A couple of years later, Selma's parents skipped town."

"With the button factory pension fund," added Lavinia.

"Leaving Selma in the lurch," said Peggy.

"Or so we thought," said Lavinia.

"However, they left Selma with an entire house full of goodies," said Peggy.

"Which she sold off piece by piece," said Lavinia.

"Until she'd raked in about two million dollars," said Peggy.

Ian let out a low whistle.

"But Stu still kept quiet about the marriage. He said Selma fed him a line about inheriting the house only if she were still single."

"That's two million reasons to keep your mouth shut," said Chuck.

"Or two million reasons for murder," said Lavinia. She turned to Ian. "We all thought Stu killed Selma for her money."

"But there wasn't any," said Peggy. "Selma lost it all in the stock market."

"Then she started putting the bite on Stu," said Lavinia. "They used to meet in a motel outside town."

"Finally Stu had enough," said Peggy. "He began seeing Virginia."

"When Stu asked Selma for a divorce, Selma demanded a big payoff," said Lavinia.

"Another reason why we were convinced that Stu killed Selma," said Peggy.

"Murder being cheaper than alimony," said Lavinia. "With Selma dead, Stu was a free man."

"How did you find out they were married?" asked Ian.

Chuck looked fondly at his wife. "Lovey and PJ started reading some old childhood books of Peggy's."

"Nancy Drew mysteries," said Lavinia.

"The next thing I knew," said Chuck, "I was living with one of the Snoop Sisters."

"Peggy started seriously sleuthing when she saw Stu at the cemetery the afternoon following Selma's funeral," said Lavinia.

"Stu buried a woman's wedding ring at Selma's grave," said Peggy.

"We thought at first that Stu had carried a torch for Selma all those years," said Lavinia.

"But the following day at Cobb House . . ."

"What's Cobb House?" asked Ian.

"The town museum," said Lavinia. "Josiah Cobb's former home. He left it to the town in his will with the provision that it become a museum."

"That Sunday afternoon Lovey and I were working as guides at the museum, when Lovey discovered a secret panel in one of the walls," said Peggy.

"We thought there might be a tunnel connecting it to Selma's house," added Lavinia.

Ian looked back and forth from Lavinia to Peggy like a spectator watching a tennis match. Chuck leaned back in his chair drinking beer, listening to the story with an amused expression on his face.

"Selma's house was originally built by Josiah Cobb as a wedding present for his daughter," said Peggy.

"There was no tunnel connecting the two houses," said Lavinia, "but we found a matching secret compartment in Selma's house. Under the trap door was a safe. Hidden in the safe was an envelope containing a marriage license and a man's wedding band."

"That's some sleuthing," said Ian.

"Right on," said Lavinia.

"When did you find all this?" asked Ian.

"Last Sunday afternoon, before the fireworks at the river," said Lavinia. "Was it only four days ago, PJ? It seems like a lifetime."

"What happened after that?" asked Ian.

"Tuesday afternoon," said Lavinia. She turned to look at Peggy. "Was it Tuesday? I've lost all track of time this week."

"It was Tuesday," said Peggy.

"Tuesday afternoon," said Lavinia, "Peggy confronted Stu at the police station and put him on suspension. That really set Virginia off. Virginia was already mad at Peggy about the teachers' raises. In retaliation, Virginia and Stu ran around town getting signatures on a petition to have Stu reinstated and Peggy ousted as mayor."

"Lovey, I forgot to ask you about that," said Peggy. "I was talking to Bob at the gas station this morning and he didn't know anything about the petition. From what Bob said, none of the regulars at Clemmie's Café knew about it either."

"We'll ask Stu," said Lavinia. "Everything's happened so fast, I'm ashamed to say I took those signatures at face value." She turned to Chuck.

"They looked real to me," said Chuck.

"I'm lost," said Ian. "Are you saying Peggy was booted out of office?"

Lavinia sighed.

"For no good reason? Without due process?"

Lavinia nodded slowly.

"We'll see about that," said Ian. "Let's get back to Stu and Selma. I want to see if I've got this straight. Stu and Selma were married. Were there any children?"

"I don't think so," said Peggy.

"I see. Stu and Selma were married," said Ian. "Selma died while they were still married. That makes Stu her heir. Was there a will?"

"We didn't find one," said Peggy. "I've got all of Selma's papers upstairs. I've been through everything. Why do you ask?"

"I was just wondering what will become of Selma's estate," said Ian. "If Stu had killed her, it would be a different story. But Selma died at Virginia's hands. It looks to me like Stu will inherit."

"Selma died flat broke," said Peggy. "All she had left was her account at the Citizen's Bank and the few furnishings left in the house."

"Which now belong to the town," said Lavinia.

"If there was no will, how did the town get into the act?" asked Ian.

"The trust," said Lavinia. "PJ, where's that trust document?"

Peggy ran to get it.

"Selma never owned the house," said Lavinia. "All she had was a life interest. Before her parents skipped town, they put the house into a trust. When Selma died, the town got the house and whatever was left in it."

Peggy returned with the trust document. She handed it to Ian. He scanned it quickly, then put it on the table. "This looks airtight to me," he said.

"But there's a hitch," said Lavinia. "We're stuck with another museum. An empty museum."

"Peggy came up with a great idea for it," said Chuck. "Tell Ian."

"Actually, Ian gave me the idea in the first place," said Peggy.

"What did I do?" asked Ian.

"When I tried to return the Cotton Mather book you gave me, you said it wasn't an original, it was a facsimile," said Peggy.

Ian nodded.

"That got me thinking. Selma left detailed descriptions and photographs of all the original furniture and paintings that were in the house. I stopped at the library Tuesday morning and did some research on period furniture. What if we recreated the original furniture for the new museum? Like the colonial signs Chuck and his students are making and selling in the store on Main Street."

"Peggy's idea was to use the new museum as a showroom for the reproduction furniture," said Chuck. "We'd set up a furniture factory right here in Cobb's Landing. There are still a lot of skilled people out of work since the button factory closed. With the new furniture factory, there would be jobs and a new industry in town."

"Peggy even thought of running tours of the furniture factory as part of Colonial Village," said Lavinia. "What do you think, Ian?"

"I think it's brilliant," said Ian. "Max will kick himself

for not having thought of it first. Where are you getting your seed money?"

"I wanted to talk to Max about that," said Peggy. "I mentioned a business loan to him, but didn't give him any details, when he stopped in Tom's Tools yesterday with a check for the town from the Colonial Village proceeds."

"What did Max say?" asked Ian.

"At first he thought I wanted to expand the hardware store," replied Peggy. "When I told Max the loan was for something else, he brushed me off, saying we needed to deal with our other problems first."

"I can guarantee you, Max will be interested now," said Ian. "I'll set up a meeting with him for tomorrow afternoon at four. Does that work for everyone?"

Peggy, Lavinia, and Chuck all nodded eagerly.

"What exactly do you do for Max?" asked Lavinia.

Ian smiled. "I'm his lawyer and investment banker."

CHAPTER 47

FRIDAY MORNING PEGGY BROKE THE NEWS TO Nicky about Virginia Morgan. She tried to soften the blow by making waffles for Nicky's breakfast. She waited to tell him the bad news until Nicky had finished eating.

"Honey, before you run off to school, there's something you should know."

"What's that, Mom?"

"Your teacher won't be there today."

"Why not?"

"Last night there was an accident at the river. Miss Morgan drowned."

"She did? How come?"

"She didn't know how to swim, Nicky."

"I thought everybody knew how to swim." Nicky was silent for a moment. "Does this mean I have to do fifth grade all over again?"

"No, honey. After today you're through with fifth grade forever."

Nicky let out a sigh of relief.

"Are you sad about Miss Morgan?"

"I'm going to have a new teacher next year anyway. Miss Morgan was kind of crabby. Except when she was being lovey-dovey with Mr. McIntyre. Now he'll have more time for baseball practice."

Charlie appeared at the kitchen door. "Hey, Nick. Did you hear about Miss Morgan? My mom said she drowned in the river because she didn't know how to swim. What a dumb thing to do. I thought teachers were supposed to be so smart. My dad's a teacher. He knows how to swim."

"Do you boys want a ride to school today? You have to clean out your desks and bring all your stuff home."

"My dad said he'd take us."

"Six hours until summer vacation starts," said Nicky. "I can't wait. See you at the carnival, Mom!"

After the boys had gone to school, Peggy and Lavinia drove to the hospital to visit Stu.

As Peggy headed out of Cobb's Landing, she said to Lavinia, "You have to call the county this morning to get someone in the police department to fill in for Stu while he's recuperating."

"Why me? That's your job."

"You forget, Lovey, I'm not the mayor. You are."

"As far as I'm concerned, it's still your job. You make the call."

"Have you ever wondered if the town made a mistake hiring Stu as the police chief?"

"Not until this week. Now I'm not so sure," said Lavinia. "I always thought of Stu as the strong, silent type. Now I think that was a cover-up for his weak character."

"I can't say he used good judgment about the women in his life."

"He picked two from the same mold. Or maybe they picked him. Think about it, PJ. Selma and Virginia weren't that different. Both were domineering and self-absorbed."

"And kept Stu under their thumbs, dancing to their tune like a puppet on a string."

"Just like old Mrs. McIntyre did when Stu was a kid."

"You're right, Lovey. I'd forgotten what a harridan Stu's mother was. She made the Wicked Witch of the West look like a fairy godmother."

Lavinia laughed. "Remember the Halloween we went over to Stu's house and wrapped all the bushes in toilet paper?"

"Then it rained, turning their yard into a mass of soggy bits of paper. They stuck to everything like glue."

"Stu didn't speak to us for a month after that because his mother made him clean up the yard instead of going to the championship football game."

"Lovey, what are we going to do? Stu didn't kill Selma, so he can't be fired for it. In two weeks he's lost his wife and his fiancée. His job is about all he's got left right now."

"Put him on paid medical leave for a month. That'll give him some time to sort himself out."

When they arrived at the hospital, Lavinia went to check on Stu's room number. She came back to the lobby with a puzzled expression on her face.

"Stu's not here, Peggy. He checked himself out a few hours ago."

"With a gunshot wound in his leg? Was he nuts?"

"C'mon, PJ. Let's track him down."

They drove back to Cobb's Landing and went immediately to Stu's house. The house was locked up tight.

Their next stop was the police station. There, too, the doors were locked, but Lavinia had a key.

After she unlocked the door, Lavinia handed the key to Peggy. "PJ, take this key back. I really don't want it."

Peggy put the key in her pocket.

On Stu's desk was a sealed envelope addressed to Peggy.

"I've got a bad feeling about this, Lovey."

Peggy opened the envelope. Inside was a letter and Stu's police badge.

Peggy sat down in Stu's desk chair and began to read.

May 29

Peggy,
I've made a real mess of everything and I'm sorry.

Sorry about the police cruiser getting burned up, sorry about everything.

Virginia killed Selma. I watched her strangle Selma in the cemetery the night Selma was supposed to meet you. Then I saw Virginia take the body down to the waterwheel. I know you thought I suspected you, I had no choice but to question you about your actions that night, and I'm sorry about that, too.

I never wanted anyone to get hurt. When I started dating Virginia, it was to make Selma jealous. But it didn't work. All Selma wanted was my money. Virginia wanted to get married. But she didn't know I couldn't marry her.

I wanted Virginia to find out I was seeing Selma. I let it slip I was meeting Selma that night, so it might as well have been my hands around Selma's neck instead of Virginia's.

With Selma dead I had no reason for not marrying Virginia. You thought putting me on suspension cost you your job as mayor. That's not true. Virginia forged the signatures on those petitions to get my job back.

I don't want to marry Virginia, so I'm getting out of Cobb's Landing before it's too late.

I know you'll do the right thing, Peggy, you always do.

Stu

"What kind of drugs did they give Stu in the hospital last night? This letter makes no sense at all. He doesn't even mention that Virginia's dead," said Peggy. "I think everyone in this town has gone mad."

"Let me see that letter," said Lavinia. "What's the date today?"

Peggy looked at the wall calendar, a freebie from Bob's gas station featuring the tire of the month. "It's Friday, May thirtieth. Why?"

"That explains everything, PJ. This letter was written yesterday, May twenty-ninth. Stu was planning to bolt all along. I bet Virginia got wind of his plans and that's what set her off. Come to think of it, she was the one doing all the talk and planning about the wedding. Stu never said much at all. Not even the night she announced their engagement."

"I stopped here yesterday afternoon on my way back to the hardware store from the post office. I wanted another look at those petitions, but the door was locked and I didn't have a key. The letter was probably sitting on Stu's desk then," said Peggy. "If I'd read it yesterday, last night would never have happened and Virginia Morgan would be alive today."

"You can't play 'what if,' PJ, it'll make you crazy. None of this—Selma, Stu, or Virginia—had anything to do with you. If Virginia Morgan were alive today, she'd be in jail for murder. Maybe it's better this way. What do you think?"

"I think we'll let Stu go and wish him well." Peggy picked up the phone.

"Who are you calling?"

"The county. Cobb's Landing needs an interim police chief to fill in until we hire someone."

CHAPTER 48

"MOM, ARE YOU READY TO GO TO THE CARNIVAL?" Nicky bounded into the hardware store with Charlie hard on his heels.

"How was your last day of school?"

"Great." Nicky fished a creased envelope out of his jeans pocket. "Here's my report card."

Peggy opened the envelope. Nicky had passed fifth grade with a solid B average. Whatever Virginia's failings or her personal differences with Peggy, she hadn't taken them out on Nicky.

Peggy hugged her son. "I'm proud of you, Nicky. You did very well this year." She opened her wallet, handed Nicky five dollars. "Go have fun at the carnival."

"Aren't you coming?"

"I have to go to a meeting at the bank, I'll see you at the carnival later."

Nicky and Charlie ran to the town square, where a small carnival, an annual event sponsored by the Cobb's Landing merchants as a school's-out treat for the students, was in progress. There were various games of chance and skill including ring toss, a baseball throw, and guess how many beans are in the jar; face-painting tables; sack races; egg and spoon races; tables with hot dogs, sodas, and ice cream; and live music by the high school band. The event would end with a public dance in the town square.

Lavinia and Chuck were waiting for Peggy at the Citizen's Bank.

Ian ushered them into Max's office.

Max breezed in, his face wreathed in a broad smile. "Sorry I'm late. A little business with a new recruit. She's wet behind the ears, but once she gets in the hot seat, she'll adjust." He rubbed his hands together briskly. "Now, Mayor, what can I do for you today? Ian said you have a business matter to discuss. He also told me about the incidents last night at the river. I'm truly sorry you were subjected to those indignities. I'm mortified that my little amusements for the tourists were put to nefarious use. I never meant you any harm. How can I make amends?"

"You can burn the stocks and the dunking stool," said Peggy.

"Consider it done. There's nothing I like better than a blazing fire. Let's get down to business, shall we?"

"Max, here's my idea," said Peggy. "We want to start a furniture factory here in Cobb's Landing."

Max listened intently while Peggy told him about the new museum and the plan to use it as a showcase for reproduction furniture, copies of the same furniture that had been in the house when it was built for Martha Cobb Martin as a bride in 1780. She showed Max some of the photographs of the original pieces and the preliminary research she'd done at the library.

"Who's going to make the sample pieces?" Max asked.

"I am," said Chuck. "Furniture building is a hobby of mine. I'm working on a side chair now. It'll be finished in a couple of weeks."

"I like this idea," said Max. "I'm sorry I didn't think of it first."

Ian winked at Peggy.

"Let's talk terms," said Max. "What do you say to two percent over prime?"

Ian shook his head.

"How about three months interest-free and two and a half percent over prime?"

"Max," said Ian. "You can do better than that."

"Who do you work for, Ian?" chided Max. He straightened his bow tie and smiled benignly. "I'm making this offer out of the goodness of my heart because I believe in the future of this wonderful town. What do you say to ten percent of the gross profits against prime plus one?"

Peggy shook her head. She'd played this game with Max before.

"All right, all right. You drive a hard bargain, Mayor. Five percent net against prime plus two and that's my final offer."

Ian nodded.

"Done," said Peggy. "Where do we sign?"

Max opened the folder sitting on his desk and passed around the promissory notes and pens. Peggy, Lavinia, and Chuck all signed on the dotted lines. In red.

Max grinned. "Now let me tell you about this nice little site I've got in mind for your factory. I'll give you a sweetheart deal on a long-term lease."

Peggy laughed. "Max, you really are a silver-tongued devil."

Max blushed, his cheeks turning redder than his bow tie. With a wink and a wave, Max left his office, humming, "Devil May Care" under his breath.

Peggy and Ian, Lavinia and Chuck all went to the town carnival to celebrate.

Later that evening, Peggy and Ian went for a walk along the Rock River. Max had kept his word. The stocks and dunking chair were history.

Peggy turned to Ian. "There's just one thing I want to know. Who *is* Max?"

Ian smiled, taking Peggy's hand in his. "That's confidential information between an attorney and client that I can't divulge. All I can say is this: You wouldn't believe me if I told you."